# Heavy Turbulence

KIMBERLY FOX

To all of the sexy pilots who can get it up
for hours
(and I'm not talking about their planes)

# ACKNOWLEDGMENTS

Thank you to everyone who helped me make this book the best that it can be.

My amazing beta readers, Lisa Bing, Scott Ryan, Kirsten Hale, Vivian Chrisman, Patricia Baxes, Bethany Quigley, Andi Downs, & Karen Proctor.

My awesome Foxy Crew review team. You don't know how much your kind words mean to me.

My editor Beverly Bernard who helped me whip this into shape.

And of course my amazing family who motivate me every day.

# CHAPTER ONE

## *RILEY*

I get shivers as I run my hand along her soft, smooth curves. She's beautiful. Sexy even. And she's my new home.

The Bombardier Global 8000.

It's the private jet of the eccentric billionaire and my new boss, Marvin Gladstone. *I wonder if she has a name. Do rich people name their planes?*

I run my hand along the bottom of the spotless white wing and get goosebumps as my fingertips run over the flaps. For an aviation dork like myself, this is better than chocolate.

My eyes take in every inch of the beauty as I inhale the sweet smell of jet exhaust from the Gulfstream G450 taxing down the runway in the distance.

"Nice," I mumble under my breath when I glance under the belly of the plane at the tires the size of my car. *Custom tires.* Not the crap Brimstone 620s that come with the model. *My new boss does things right.*

"Don't touch my plane!" someone snaps from behind me, and I jerk my hand back like I just touched a hot oven.

Hot redness creeps up my neck and into my cheeks as I turn around with a guilty face. Mr. Gladstone is walking over with his shoulders squared back and a pissed off look on his face. His stunning wife is walking behind him staring at her phone and looking completely disinterested as a man in a chauffeur outfit walks behind both of them carrying all of their luggage.

"Who let you in here?" Mr. Gladstone barks as he approaches. My voice seizes in my throat, and I involuntarily take a step back almost bumping into his precious plane.

It's only us inside the private hangar at LAX airport. I glance over at the chauffeur, and he gives me a look of sympathy. I'm sure he knows what it feels like to get yelled at by rich people. *At least I'm not alone.*

He quickly drops the bags and scurries out while giving me a look that can only mean 'good luck.'

*Shit.*

"I'm the new stewardess," I say, finally finding my voice, but it's squeakier and has more cracks than normal. "Remember, Mr. Gladstone? You hired me a month ago."

"Oh," he says, the angry look on his face disappearing as fast as it came. "Of course. Kylie."

"It's Riley," I correct him as I straighten my jacket.

He twists his face up and looks at me funny. "Are you sure?"

"Pretty sure. But you can call me whatever you like," I say with a nervous chuckle.

That finally gets his wife's attention, and she snaps her bright green eyes up at me, locking them on mine like heat-seeking missiles. They're brimming with hate.

Kara Gladstone.

Hidden Pleasures lingerie model. Wife of a billionaire. All around bitch if I'm to believe the many media reports, which right now, looking into her sinister eyes, I do.

She flips her wavy blonde hair behind her shoulders and flexes her toned arms as she crosses them over her spectacular fake tits. She slowly looks me up and down.

I gulp even though I have nothing to gulp about. I'm not going to be anything but professional with her husband, and anyway, I suck at flirting. My attempts at flirting always come across as awkward and stiff, leaving the guy walking away with his head shaking, wondering what just happened.

Mr. Gladstone steps in for a hug, swallowing me in his bear-like arms. He's a wide, stocky man with a lot of muscle under a layer of fat and thick hair. He has the body of a former college football player who turned in his cleats for slippers.

"Welcome to the family," he says, crushing me as Kara stares me down with an intense glare.

I take a much-needed breath as he lets me go. "This is my wife, Kara," he says, turning to show his silicone trophy.

She reaches out for a handshake, and I hold my breath as I slide my hand into hers. A little whimper escapes my throat as she clamps down on it, crushing my fingers in her CrossFit grip. "Nice to meet you," she says through clenched teeth.

*She's going to be a problem.*

"Come," Mr. Gladstone says, grabbing my arm and pulling me away. "This is my plane." He points up to it, and my heart starts beating fast when I look into the huge Flat Rated engines that are capable of sixteen thousand, five hundred pounds of thrust. *This is so exciting.*

Mr. Gladstone starts telling me about the aircraft, but I already know everything about it. I love planes. I nod and pretend like I'm learning it all for the first time. He's enthusiastic and full of life when he talks, moving his hands animatedly as he nods his head and smiles. He's a handsome man, in his mid-fifties with wisps of gray on the sides of his dark hair. He has a nice smile and fierce brown eyes that command your attention, which I'm sure is one of the reasons why he has a ten-figure bank account.

"Where are we going today?" I ask when he's done showing me around the plane. Kara disappeared into it a few minutes ago.

"The Cayman Islands," he says, rubbing the salt and pepper stubble on his thick jaw. "I have a meeting with Prince Kalib of Pertoria. Trying to sell him a fleet of yachts. Word on the street is he's looking to buy sixty. One for each of the girls in his harem."

I shake my head in disbelief. I've stepped into a new world; the world of billionaires and unlimited money. Much different from my world of late rent and double coupon days. I better get used to it. In my world, we buy generic brand aluminum paper and stock up on our favorite gum when it goes on sale for eleven cents off. Yachts and private jets are not things that are normally in my broke little universe.

"Well, good luck," I say as we head toward the steps leading into the plane. "I hope you make the sale."

"I don't need luck," he says, puffing out his wide chest. "I made my first million while I was in high school and my first billion when I was thirty-four. If there's one thing I'm good at, it's selling."

His enthusiasm is contagious, and I can't help but smile. I knew this job would be great. Following around a billionaire to exotic locations with the best of everything. Five-star hotels and restaurants. Limousines and yachts. I can't wait to see all of the sights. I've never been anywhere, and Marvin Gladstone is known to travel to the best spots in the Caribbean, Europe, and Asia, and I get to go with him.

My eyes dart to my watch. We're scheduled to leave at nine forty-six, and I would like to make sure that the galley and cabin are ready for the flight. "Should we head inside?"

Mr. Gladstone nods. "Let's go make some money!"

My grin widens and my pulse races as I walk up the steps into the aircraft. Adrenaline pumps through my body with every step that I take. This is my dream job. Well, actually my dream job would be the one behind the controls in the cockpit, but this is good too.

Mr. Gladstone disappears into the fuselage as I step inside with wide eyes. Talk about luxury. The hardwood floors alone are probably worth more than my condo. I glance down into the cabin, and Kara is sitting cross-legged on one of the large leather seats that look like La-Z-Boys, flipping the magazine on her lap with an annoyed look on her face.

Her eyes dart up to mine, and I turn around quickly before she can scowl at me. My heart thumps as I stare open mouthed at the cockpit. There are so many lights and buttons. This is what a gambler must feel like when they walk into a casino or a little kid staring at his unopened presents on Christmas morning.

I want to touch everything. I want to slide into the leather Captain's seat, slip the headphones over my ears, and grab the yoke. I've spent so many hours on my computer flying planes in my favorite aircraft simulation game that I could probably take-off and land it without a problem.

I dip my head under the low door of the cockpit and inhale the sweet smell of leather and grease. I'm in heaven. I love cockpits.

That word always makes me shake my head. Only in a male-dominated industry would something be called a cockpit. I'll never understand men. You don't hear nurses calling a prep room a pussy pit.

"Pretty cool, huh?" Mr. Gladstone asks, sneaking up on me. I nearly jump out of my stewardess uniform, the one with the excessively short skirt.

"It's amazing," I say, admiring all of the instruments.

"It was a little birthday gift to myself," he says with a wide smile.

"Where are the pilots?" I ask, checking my watch again. We're supposed to be leaving in twelve minutes, and a plane like this takes at least half an hour to perform all of the necessary safety checks before take-off.

"Dex?" he asks with a shrug of his wide shoulders. "Who the fuck knows? Probably sticking his dick in the female security agent who was in charge of patting him down."

"What?" I ask, jerking my head back in confusion.

He pushes past me and slips into the Captain's chair. "I can start it," he says, flicking on random switches. The lights on the flight deck begin to light up, and the ground under me hums after he turns the engines on.

I rub the back of my sweaty neck as I lean in. "Should you be touching all of that?" I ask with a cracking voice. Only an experienced and licensed pilot should be in that chair.

"Probably not," he says, flicking a switch over his head that causes a grinding sound from somewhere behind me.

I bite my nails and head into the galley. The nerves rushing through my veins are making my stomach roll, and my mouth is so dry that I can't even lick my lips. This is too much to handle. I like when things are by the book, and having my unqualified boss fudging around with the controls is making me want to use the airsick bags even though the plane hasn't left the runway yet.

"Wow," I gasp when I walk into the galley. It makes me forget about Mr. Gladstone playing around in the cockpit, almost. The galley is just as nice as the rest of the plane, with smooth granite countertops and a large stainless steel fridge. It's first class all the way.

There's a small bar filled with bottles of alcohol that I've never heard of, but they all look expensive. A Porto from Italy with the old faded label curling up in the corner. A whiskey from Ireland that's written in what looks like Gaelic. The date on the bottle is eighteen sixty-two. It smells like paint thinner.

The thump of shoes walking up the metal steps outside makes me flinch, and I place the old bottle of whiskey back on the glass shelf. It's one of the pilots. He walks into the plane, and I try to busy myself, looking in the cupboards and fridge, making sure that everything is stocked up. I don't want to look like a slacker in front of my co-worker, even if *he* is the one who's late.

"What the hell, Marv?" he says, his deep masculine voice giving me warm shivers. "Get out of my office!"

Mr. Gladstone chuckles. "I was just warming her up for you," he says as he heads into the cabin where his wife is waiting.

"Do I look like I need help warming a girl up?" he calls out with a hint of annoyance in his voice.

I take a deep breath and smooth out my uniform, pulling up my top which keeps trying to show more cleavage than I want it to and pulling down my skirt which is ridiculously short. The uniform looks like it was designed by a teenage boy. Way more sexy than professional.

I bend over and take a quick glance at my blurry reflection in the stainless-steel fridge. My brown hair is pulled tight behind my head with my hat secured firmly on top. No lipstick on my teeth.

I'm good to go.

I push down my nerves and walk back to the cockpit to introduce myself to the pilot. I really want to keep this job and am nervous to make a good first impression, which is not one of my strengths. I usually babble on awkwardly while the person I'm meeting stares at me with confusion in their eyes, or worse, pity.

He's sitting in the cockpit with the light blue sleeves of his tight shirt rolled up his thick tattooed forearms as he presses some buttons on the flight deck.

"Hi," I say, my voice coming out like a timid mouse.

He turns and his crystal blue eyes hit me like a punch in the gut. He grins as he drags his mischievous eyes down to my skirt which is hiked up my thighs, dangerously close to the bottom of my ass cheeks.

I don't even move. He's stunningly gorgeous. His bright eyes pop against the contrast of his short, dark brown hair and tanned skin. His pilot cap is tilted on his head, and his tie is loose around his muscular neck like he doesn't give a fuck.

His sexy lips curl up into a smile and I gulp a little too loud. His face is beautiful with sharp cheekbones and a short-cropped beard covering the hard line of his jaw. I had an image of an older pilot in my head, so it catches me off guard when I see this beautiful specimen who is the epitome of a confident male, leaning back in the seat, fucking me with his eyes.

"Hi," he answers with a velvety voice that makes my knees turn to Play-Doh. "Dex," he says, sticking out his hand.

"Riley," I say as I slide my hand into his. He grins as he squeezes it, giving me just enough pressure to let me know that he's the boss. I just hope my palms aren't too sweaty.

He has an edge to his look. He's not like any pilot that I've ever seen before and trust me, I've seen a lot. I used to collect pilot baseball cards. Samuel Goldstein Rookie Card. Ron Willard Sunshine Airlines MVP. He flew fourteen thousand, three hundred and sixteen hours in nineteen-ninety-seven! Yes, I'm that much of an aviation nerd.

"It's nice to meet you," I say, taking my hand back when he finally releases it. "Where's your co-pilot?"

He chuckles. "You're looking at him."

I jerk my head back in surprise. "But this is a multi-crew aircraft," I say, shaking my head. "The FAA requires that all jet air transport aircrafts have at least two pilots."

Dex smirks. "That's a bullshit law. I can fly this thing while taking a nap. It's on auto-pilot the whole time."

"Auto-pilot has been known to fail," I say, straightening my shoulders as my voice speeds up. "We really should have another pilot."

"Well, we don't," he says with a shrug. "Is the cabin ready for take-off?"

My hands clench into fists so tight that my knuckles burn. "It will be," I say as my stomach hardens.

He turns and flicks on a switch which makes the ground under my feet vibrate even more. "Better hurry up. We're leaving in sixty."

"An hour?" I ask, checking my watch. "We're already late."

"Not sixty minutes," he says with a grin. "Sixty seconds."

My mouth drops open in shock. "You haven't done any of the pre-flight checks."

He huffs out a frustrated breath. "You worry about the coffee. I'll worry about the plane."

I'm clenching my jaw so tight that my teeth feel like they're about to shatter as we stare each other down. He gives me a little wink, and I spin on my heels and storm off into the galley with heat flushing through my body.

*Why are hot guys always the most frustrating?*

I'm whipping out the in-flight lunch and slamming cupboards in such a heated rage that I don't even hear him slip into the galley behind me. He slides his hand along my sweaty lower back and I let out a scream.

"Wound a little tight?" he asks with a laugh as he opens the fridge. "Is that why you're named Riley? Because you're all riled up?"

I slam the fridge door closed with his hand still on the handle, and he looks at me with an amused expression on his arrogant face. His beautiful, sexy, arrogant face.

"What are you doing here?" I snap. "*I* worry about the coffee. *You* worry about the plane. Isn't that what you said?"

He opens the fridge door easily even though I'm pushing on it as hard as I can, trying to keep it closed. He's big. A head taller than me with broad muscular shoulders and a full chest that's hiding behind his tight pilot's shirt. "I'm not here for coffee," he says, reaching into the fridge.

"Oh, hell no!" I yell when I see what he took. A cold can of beer.

He cracks it open and winks at me as he takes a sip.

I'm shaking with anger. "That is against so many Federal regulations," I say, sweeping my arms wildly as I talk. "It's dangerous and just plain irresponsible."

He chuckles as he turns and walks back to the cockpit. "That's what makes it so good." He raises the beer over his shoulder and tilts the can like he's toasting me from across the room.

"No, no, no, no, no, no," I mutter to myself as my nostrils flare and my muscles quiver. I'm not being an accessory to this. I'm doing the responsible thing. The mature thing. The decent thing.

I'm telling.

I storm into the cabin and walk right up to Mr. Gladstone with my chin held high. "Sir," I say with a shaking voice. "I regret to inform you that the pilot of this aircraft is drinking beer in the cockpit."

"What?" Mr. Gladstone yells, jumping out of his seat. He storms past me into the front of the plane, and I can't help but smirk as the arrogant, cocky pilot is about to get his ass handed to him by our boss. I'm giddy with anticipation as I follow him.

"What the hell?" Mr. Gladstone yells at the entrance of the cockpit.

Dex looks over his shoulder at us. His eyes dart down to my legs when he sees me and an angry flood of heat rushes into my chest. I've always had a thing for pilots but this arrogant ass is probably going to cure me of that.

"What's up, Marv?" he asks, sounding like he doesn't have a care in the world. His lack of giving any fucks is really getting to me. I'm really going to enjoy this.

"Why are you drinking my beer?" Mr. Gladstone asks, sounding pissed off. "You know that's my favorite beer, and I only have one case left. Drink the scotch. I bought it for you!"

"Sorry, boss," Dex says, grinning at me as he takes another sip. "Want to ride shotgun?"

"Yeah!" Mr. Gladstone says, jumping into the empty seat which is supposed to be reserved for a licensed, qualified pilot and not a crazy billionaire who probably has had no formal training.

"Sir," I say, giving it one last try. "I don't think this is all very wise. If even a fraction of his reaction speed is affected by the depressive effects of alcohol, we could crash."

Mr. Gladstone shrugs as he slips on the green headset. "You don't become a self-made billionaire by being afraid of taking chances."

Dex shoots me a smirk as he shakes the empty can, as if I'm going to get him another one. I give him the finger instead.

I turn and head to the seat in the hallway to strap myself in for the take-off when Mr. Gladstone calls me back. "Riley," he says as the plane jerks forward and Dex begins to taxi out of the hangar. "Bring us a couple of beers, would ya."

My body stiffens, and all I can do is shake my head as I head to the fridge like a zombie and bring back two beers. The engines are rumbling, and our airplane is rolling toward the runway where another jet is taking off.

Dex flashes his straight white teeth at me as he takes the beers out of my stiff hands.

"Buckle up," he says with a grin. "It's going to be a bumpy ride."

# CHAPTER TWO

## *RILEY*

The view from up here always gives me goosebumps. The fluffy shape of the clouds. Being closer to the sun than humans were ever intended to be. I love it. But not today. I'm too busy biting my nails and cursing out Dex under my breath.

The jet seems to have steadied in the air and settled on its heading. I just hope it's not headed straight into a mountain.

I unbuckle my belt and try to pull my skirt down as I stand up. This thing is like a rubber band, and it flies back up my legs. *Fuck it.* I'm too annoyed to care anymore.

Kara is sitting in the cabin by herself, and I head over to see if she would like anything. A fashion magazine is draped over her knee, and she's clutching a blue pen in her hand, drawing a mustache onto the beautiful model who's posing in a bikini. The word 'bitch' is scratched over the model's body so hard that the C is torn through the page.

"Would you like a beverage, Mrs. Gladstone?" I ask with my hands folded in front of me. "Maybe a hot towel or a snack?"

"There is something I would like," she says, drawing little X's over the eyes in the picture.

"Anything," I say, holding my breath.

Her wicked amber eyes slide up my body, and she sneers when she meets my eye. "I would like you to stop being such a little whore around my husband."

"What?" I gasp, stepping back in shock.

"You heard me," she says, glaring at me. "Walking around with your short skirt and letting him touch you like that. I know what you're doing."

My hands fly to my skirt, and I self-consciously try to inch it down, but the stubborn material is refusing to move.

"He just touched my shoulder," I say defensively.

"Do you know how long it took me to snag a billionaire?" she asks as she slowly rips the page out of her magazine and crumples it into a ball. "Four years. That's four years of laughing at his stupid jokes, four years of pretending I like blow jobs, and four years of being bored out of my mind."

"It sounds like you two are really in love," I say, staring back at her.

She tosses the crumpled-up ball at me but misses. "Stay the fuck away from him."

"Yes, ma'am," I say, turning and heading back to the galley. I lean against the counter and close my eyes tight, trying to keep the tears in that are struggling to burst from my lids.

It wasn't supposed to be this way. This was supposed to be the closest thing to my dream job.

Ever since I was a kid, I always wanted to be a pilot. When I was six, I had airplane pajamas, airplane sheets, and I dressed up as a pilot on Halloween for six years in a row. But when I graduated high school, my mom didn't have the fifty grand necessary to send me to pilot school, so I scrounged together five grand and went to flight attendant school instead.

It was the next best thing. Or so I thought.

The overhead speakers crackle and Dex's deep voice comes on, the sexy timbre making my heart speed up. *"Paging hot waitress, paging hot waitress,"* he says, making my teeth grind. My dentist is going to love this guy.

*"Your two sexy pilots are very thirsty,"* he continues.

*Are they already finished the beers?!?*

*"We're requesting some champagne to celebrate the successful take-off."*

I rip the door of the fridge open and take a deep breath of the cold air as I stare at the special edition bottle of Dom Perignon inside. I'd be surprised if it didn't cost more than my car. *Fuck that.* I'm not giving them any more alcohol. I reach past the bottle to a can of ginger ale in the back, crack it open, and pour it into two champagne flutes.

"There she is," Dex says, grinning at me over his muscular shoulder as I walk up to the entrance of the cockpit with the ginger ale on a tray. His smooth lips part, showing a flash of his straight white teeth. "You didn't bring one for yourself? I thought we could party."

I look past him through the windshield to the

white clouds that are inching closer on their way behind us. "You thought wrong," I hiss, feeling my chest tighten.

He glances down at my legs and smirks. "You look like you're here to party."

Mr. Gladstone's phone rings and he walks to the back of the plane to answer it, leaving the two of us alone.

"I didn't choose this skirt," I say, trying to tug it down while balancing the tray with the two top-heavy champagne flutes on it. Not an easy task. Especially when my annoying skirt refuses to cooperate.

"Maybe not," he says, biting his lip as he shamelessly stares at my bare legs. "But that skirt sure chose you. And I'm glad that it did."

I shake my head in frustration. "Shouldn't you keep your eyes on where you're going?"

"I am," he says, flashing me a confident grin. "I'm going between those sexy legs as soon as we land. Or now, if you'd prefer?"

"I'd prefer if you kept your eyes on your flight instruments instead of getting drunk and sexually harassing me." I glare at him, pretending the redness in my cheeks is from anger and not from the sexual invitation that he just threw down between us.

He reaches for a champagne flute, and I jerk the tray away from his hand. "Are you even qualified to fly this plane?"

Dex snorts out a laugh. "This fucking thing?" he says, twisting his face up like he's offended. "I used to fly an F-22 Raptor in the US military. Flying this thing is like riding a tricycle after years of doing wheelies on a motorcycle while going three hundred miles per hour."

My gaze turns from angry to incredulous. *He was in the Air Force? Flying F-22s?*

I'm so jealous. The F-22 Raptor is one of my favorite planes.

"I can fly this thing in my sleep," he says with a shrug of his strong shoulders. "Now, can you hand me my champagne before I die of boredom? If I have to stare at another cloud, I'm going to kill myself."

"No," I say firmly, locking my eyes back onto his. "You're not drinking alcohol again while I'm on board."

"The parachute is over there," he answers, motioning to the back wall with his bright blue eyes.

I don't take my eyes off him. "You don't have to be such a dick about it. I'm in charge here too," I say. The safety of all passengers on board is the flight crew's responsibility. *My* responsibility.

"That's where you're wrong," he says, his icy blue eyes dropping to my feet. My eyes sink down to where he's looking. I'm standing on the metal floor of the cockpit, past the clear line of the hardwood floors.

"*My* cockpit. *My* rules," he says, drawling out the word *cock* in his sexy voice. The way he says it just rolls off his tongue like velvet. "And while you're in *my* cockpit, you'll do as *I* say."

"You know, you're really full of yourself," I say, crinkling my nose up at him in disgust.

He grins. "You should be full of me too."

"Ugh," I say, spinning on my heels to get out of his frustrating presence.

"Wait," he calls out. I hate myself for stopping and turning, but I do. There's something about him though. Maybe it's the fact that he's a pilot, or maybe it's the tattoos spread over his thick forearms that are hot as fuck, but I feel him getting under my skin. I feel like I'm back at the playground in elementary school and attracted to Nathan Miller who keeps pulling my hair and throwing sand in my face. Hating him for doing it, but loving the attention he's giving me.

"What?" I hiss.

"You forgot my champagne."

It's only ginger ale, but there's no way he's getting it. I glance down at the hardwood floors that I'm standing on. "*My* cabin. *My* rules."

"You're sexy when you're mad," he says with a sly grin.

My cheeks are heating up again. I hate how he can do that so easily.

I squeeze my free hand into a fist and bite my bottom lip as my pulse races. *Why does he have to be so hot? And in that pilot uniform…*

"I'm not mad," I lie through gritted teeth. Why do I even bother denying it? I'm easier to read than a coloring book.

"Good," he says, rolling his sleeve up his round tattooed bicep. "Then we can be friends."

His lips curl up into a smile, and I take a deep breath. "You want to be friends?"

"Are you a member of the mile-high club?" he asks, ignoring my question.

"What?" I ask, jerking my head back.

He grins. "Have you ever had sex in an airplane?"

"I know what it means," I snap back. "It's just… Why are you asking me that?"

His grin alone must have gotten him laid

dozens of times. "These flights are long," he says with a raised eyebrow.

"They're going to feel like an eternity if you're the only one that I have to talk to," I say.

"Just wait," he says, dipping his chin down. "You think this job is fun because we're headed to the Caribbean right now. Wait until Marv heads to Pakistan and we're stuck in a cheap motel for five weeks while he wines and dines the ambassador."

I nearly drop the tray. I was so excited for this job and thinking of all of the exotic destinations that a billionaire would go to that I forgot the main reason why a billionaire would want a private jet in the first place: for business.

"Or wait until we go to his favorite hunting spot in the middle of winter."

I gulp. "I'm afraid to ask."

"Mongolia," he says, shuddering with the thought. "Fucking Mongolia. He dragged me there for three weeks last winter, the fucking prick."

"What does he hunt in Mongolia?" I ask. I thought it was just miles and miles of plains and rolling hills.

"He hunts rabbits," he says with a chuckle. "With a fucking hawk. He loves that shit. Meanwhile, we'll be sitting in a crappy motel watching Mongolian soap operas, bored out of our minds. It won't be so boring if we could be doing other things."

"Other things?" I ask. This time it's my turn to raise an eyebrow.

"Other things," he says with a nod of his sharp jaw. "Which brings me back to my original question. Have you ever been fucked on an airplane?"

My cheeks redden as my breath quickens.

He's playing with me. He's trying to get under my skin, and it's working. Well, two can play at that game. It's time to fuck with him back.

"Sounds like a boring job," I say as he takes a long glance at my chest. "What did you do to get kicked out of the Air Force and get stuck with a shitty job like this?"

He huffs out a breath and narrows his eyes at me. I hit a sore spot. Score one for Riley!

"I bet you love to get wild," he says, ignoring my question and trying to get the upper hand back. "I bet I could get you sopping wet with one flick of my wrist."

"*You* get *me* wet?" I say with a snort of laughter. The champagne flutes on the tray clink together, and I steady my hand. "You couldn't get me wet even if we crashed into the ocean, which seems to be a real possibility since you can't seem to go five minutes without a drink. Now tell me why you got kicked out of the Air Force."

"Come sit on my lap and I'll tell you all about it," he says, patting his black pants.

I'm tempted but I hold my ground.

"I'd rather use the parachute," I say with my fiercest glare.

"Afraid you'll get wet?" he asks in a deep, raspy voice with a grin on his sexy lips. "One flick of the wrist. It's all it will take."

"What did I tell you?" I ask, holding my chin up high. "You couldn't get me wet if you had a—"

Dex flicks his wrist of the hand that's holding the yoke and the plane lurches up, spilling the two champagne flutes on my tray. The ginger ale lands all over my shirt, soaking me in sticky soda.

"Oops," he says, staring at me with a cocky grin. "Told you I could get you wet."

I rush forward with murder in my eyes, and he quickly closes the door of the cockpit, locking it from the other side. I can hear the prick laughing.

He's a dead man.

# CHAPTER THREE

## *DEX*

"Sorry for that little bump of turbulence," I say over the PA system of the jet. "I was testing out my sexy new stewardess, and things got a little crazy as you can see. She left the cockpit dripping wet."

I release the button on the PA while laughing as I picture her all pissed off in the cabin. I wait for it, and sure enough, four seconds later she knocks on the door and gives me a "fuck you" from the other side.

I shift in my seat and grin as I picture her all worked up in the bathroom, sliding off her wet uniform, cursing me as she strips down to her wet bra. "Mmmm," I moan, getting hard in my pants.

Riley is gorgeous with her heated green eyes and her brown hair pulled back as tight as her ass. That short skirt is killing me the way it hugs the top of her slender legs, making me wonder how soft the insides of her thighs would feel squeezed against my cheeks as I bury my tongue deep inside of her.

She's feisty, just how I like it. I love the way she keeps raising her dainty little nose in defiance and acting like she's not squirming inside at my crude words. But those rosy cheeks that are so quick to blush keep betraying her coolness.

I have to entertain myself somehow on these long trips. These boring fucking clouds won't do it.

As much as I'm fucking with her, I'm stoked to have her on board. Finally, someone I can play with. Not like the last stewardess, Rose. What a snorefest she was.

Playing games and making Riley uncomfortable on her first day is a bit of an asshole move, but it's the quickest way to get a woman in bed, or on the floor, or in the cockpit. Making a few dirty comments to get under a woman's skin always jacks up the sexual tension, and when they finally give in, they unleash all of that frustrated energy onto my cock. A quick angry fuck with no desire to settle down. It always works like a charm.

Riley doesn't know what she's in for. I already got her all worked up and fuming. She's probably thinking about me right now as she undresses, cursing me and wanting to make me pay.

But I might have underestimated her. She got under my skin as well.

I rub my jaw as I regret bringing up my time in the Air Force. Usually throwing out that I was a fighter jet pilot is enough to get the panties down, but Riley seemed to have caught on that I was kicked out. It backfired, and she went for my nuts instead.

My dishonorable discharge is still a sore spot for me. I loved that job. Flying a fighter jet at fifteen hundred miles per hour was the ultimate rush. And I was good at it. So yeah, the discharge pissed me off.

It still does, so I wasn't about to explain to *her* what happened.

I've been stuck with this job ever since, flying around this slow-moving bus for the past year and a half. Marv is cool when he's not being a dick and making me stay in Siberia for weeks at a time while he tries to get a pipeline installed through some poor fuck's farm.

The image of Riley's soft lips tightened into an angry grimace is running through my mind again when there's a knock on the door. *She's back for more.*

"Come in," I call out with a smile brewing on my lips. Time for round two.

But it's not Riley. It's my other conquest: Kara.

She's looking sinfully hot as usual with a tight low-cut dress that can barely contain her ample tits. She licks her lips when she sees me, and it's enough to get me rock hard.

"Hi, Dexy," she says, laying on the little girl voice extra hard. *Uh-oh. She wants something.*

Her perfect blonde hair is feathered around her slim shoulders and she's got that pouty look on her face. The one that drives me wild.

Kara is stunning, and I'm embarrassed that I haven't gotten anywhere with her yet. She's the ultimate jackpot. Hidden Pleasures model. Boss' wife. So taboo. So off limits. So fucking hot.

"What can I do for you, my love?" I ask, flashing her a wide smile.

She slides her delicate hand over my shoulder and leans down, tickling my cheek with her silky hair.

Her vanilla perfume has my head swirling and my dick hardening, and the front row view of her voluptuous cleavage beside me isn't helping.

I want her bad and she knows it. She toys with me. Always dangling a carrot in front of me and then yanking it back when I reach for it. She's a master cock tease of the highest order.

And one day she will be mine.

"I don't like this new girl," she whispers. Her warm breath that smells like cinnamon washes over me, and I can't help but wonder what the rest of her smells like. "I want her gone."

"Why are you asking me?" I say, shifting in my seat. My sudden hard-on is making these pants feel awfully tight. "Why don't you ask the big man?"

She licks her lips as she traces her fingertips down my chest and over my abs. I swallow hard as she passes my belt buckle and slides her hand down my thigh, barely missing my hard cock. "We both know who the *real* big man is on this plane."

"What's in it for me?" I ask with a grin.

My dick jumps as she takes her hand off my leg and stands back up. "Make her disappear, and you'll find out." She's staring at me with 'fuck me' eyes, but one thing I've learned is that Kara is a master at giving 'fuck me' eyes and not really meaning it. All this woman really craves is money. That's the only thing that gets her hot.

But I'm still going to try. I'll never stop trying with her.

She struts to the open door of the cockpit, swaying her luscious round hips with every step. She stops at the door and leans on the frame like it's a stripper pole. "Make her gone," she repeats in a husky voice, "and my panties may follow her."

My heart is pounding so hard that I can't hear her stiletto heels clicking and clacking as she struts away.

I stare at the hovering clouds wondering if she's telling the truth or if it's just another dangling carrot when Marv walks in and plops himself down on the co-pilot's seat.

"Where are we?" he asks, flicking a switch that he shouldn't be touching. I slap his hand away.

"Somewhere over Texas," I say, checking the GPS. "Want to land and get some Tex-Mex?"

Marv rubs his belly and groans. "Don't tempt me. Do they have a drive-through at the Houston airport?"

"It will take too long to land with all of the line-ups," I say, getting hungry. (The stewardess hasn't brought me any snacks. I wonder why…) "I can land this thing in the parking lot of Cheesy's."

Marv grins. "Some other time. I have business to take care of."

"What are you up to now?"

Marv's face lights up with an enthusiastic smile. Nothing gets him happier than making money. "Trying to unload sixty yachts on a prince." He lets out a booming laugh. "It would be the biggest yacht sale in history."

I grin. "Sounds like a good time to ask for a raise."

He winces. "Money's been tight lately. All of my liquidity is tied up in the Siberian pipeline."

I can't help but laugh. What a cheap fuck. He's got billions sitting in dozens of bank accounts across the globe, he owns over twenty companies, nine of them are in the Fortune 500, and his watch costs more than my parents made in their lifetime. But ask him for an inflation-based raise, and suddenly his pockets are empty and he doesn't have a pot to jerk off in.

"Fine," I say, rubbing my chin. "Then let me ask you for something else."

"Anything," he says. *Yeah, as long as it's not money.*

I take a deep breath and hold the air in, letting it burn my throat. "Hire another stewardess. This one is not going to cut it." It feels wrong as I say it, and I immediately regret it.

"I need her for something," he says, looking at me sideways.

Anger flashes through me. If he's trying to fuck her, he's going to have to go through me. I grip the yoke with white knuckles as I wait for him to go on.

"And I need *you*," he continues.

"For what?"

Marv shifts in his seat. "I need you and her to pretend like you're happy owners of one of my yachts."

*Happy customers?* I stifle a laugh. Everyone knows his yachts are pieces of shit.

"Why?"

"For the social proof," Marv explains. "It's a powerful psychological trick I always use for selling. Why do you think companies bend over backward to get reviews? Why do you think McDonald's says over ninety-nine billion served? For the social proof. That's what you two are going to provide for the prince."

29

I shrug my shoulders. "No problem." I never question Marv when it comes to selling. His bank account alone is proof that he knows what he's doing.

"You'll be our friends we're traveling with, but that's not all," he says as he reaches out to touch another button on the dash. The look I shoot him makes his hand recoil. "The prince is big on family. It would be better if you two pretend that you're married."

"You *two?*" I repeat with a raised eyebrow.

"You and Riley."

"HA!" This is getting better and better. "I'll do it under two conditions."

"What are they?"

"I get to be there when you tell her." I'm grinning so hard that my cheeks hurt. I can't wait to see the look of anger on her face when Marv tells her that she has to act like my wife. It's going to be epic.

"Done," he says while he adjusts the special edition Rolex on his wrist. Marv claims the watch was a gift from Obama, but I saw him buy it in Dubai. "What's the second condition?"

This is probably a bad idea but it feels so right. "Cancel Riley's room reservation at the hotel."

He dips his head as he turns to me. "You want her to sleep in the parking lot?"

I shake my head. "I want to share a room with her. Break her in a bit. Plus, why would a married couple stay in different rooms? It's safer this way."

"She hates you," he says, crossing his arms over his massive chest. "Why would you want to put yourself through that misery?"

I turn back to the clouds. "Just hook it up."

He shrugs. "You're insane."

"And you're addicted to money," I respond as he thinks about it. "I'll play nice. Sixty yachts, Marv."

He turns to me with dollar signs in his greedy eyes. "Done." He shakes my hand and nods. "You help me get the sale, and I'll get rid of Riley after," he says with a coldness to his voice. "You can pick whichever stripper you want as a stewardess after."

I sigh heavily as my stomach suddenly feels knotted. I shouldn't have asked for Riley to be fired, but the image of Kara's delicious tits in my face is still lingering in my mind, overriding my better judgment. Tits usually have that effect on me.

I'm about to tell him that maybe we should give her another chance when he leans toward the door, about to call her over.

"Let me," I say, grabbing the handset of the PA system. I click the button and raise it to my smirking mouth. "Paging, Miss Wet T-shirt Contest. Please report to the cock, pit." My voice rings out through the speakers, and I hear her let out an "ugh" from the galley.

She storms over with her gorgeous face twisted in anger, but she stops dead when she sees Marv sitting beside me.

"Hello, Mr. Gladstone," she says, looking everywhere but at me. "Can I get you anything *non-alcoholic* while you're up here in the cockpit?"

Her body is tense, and her jaw is shut so tight that it would take a crowbar to open it. I chuckle when I look down at her shirt all wrinkled up, probably from drying it with the hand dryer in the bathroom. It still looks good pressed against her full chest, and the thought of her standing topless in the bathroom while she dried it is getting me going again.

"How is your first day going?" Marv asks her, ignoring her question.

She huffs out a breath and glances at me for half a second with a look that would send a wild tiger scurrying away in fear. The angry heat from her eyes is so hot that I have to check the altimeter to make sure we're not flying directly into the sun. We're good.

"It's great," she says with a voice so tight that it sounds like it's about to snap. And looking at the way her rigid shoulders are thrust back, the way her hands are clenched into fists, and the way the cute little vein on her neck is popping out, I can tell that she is dangerously close to snapping.

"This is a rather, how do I say this," Marv says, scratching his chin as he looks up at the ceiling, "*unconventional* job."

Riley glances over at me nervously as she waits for the reason why this job is so 'unconventional.' I can't imagine what she's thinking right now, but the tiny blonde hairs on her arms are standing straight up.

"Sometimes I'm going to ask you to do some things to help out the business," he says, waving his hands while he explains it.

"*Okay,*" she says warily. She has barely taken a breath since she arrived.

"As I mentioned," Marv goes on, "I have a potential sale for some yachts."

She nods. "With Prince Kalib."

"Right," Marv says, snapping his fingers. "Well, he's really big on family."

"The guy with the sixty-woman harem is big on family?" she asks as she rolls her eyes. "Makes sense."

"I just need a small favor," Marv says. I bite my tongue in anticipation to see her reaction. She's going to flip.

"What is it?" she asks, subconsciously taking a step back.

Marv takes in a breath. "I need you to pretend that you're married."

She glances at me with nervous eyes and then takes another step back. "To who?"

Marv presents me with his hands like a Barker Beauty presenting the world's shittiest prize. "With Dex."

She crosses her arms over those beautiful breasts and glares at me. "I'd rather eat glass."

Marv drops his head in frustration. He curses under his breath before raising his head back up with a wide smile on his lips. "It would mean a lot to me."

Riley turns her head and seems to be looking for something behind her.

"What are you doing?" Marv asks.

"Looking for that parachute," she answers.

"Better jump fast," I say with a grin. "We're going to be over the Gulf of Mexico shortly."

"I'll make it worth your while," Marv says. My ears perk up. So do hers. "I'll give you an extra vacation day."

She laughs. "I want a ten percent commission."

Marv jerks his head back like he's been slapped. I stare at Riley in awe. I didn't know she had it in her. It makes me wonder what else I had wrong about her.

"Point one percent," Marv answers, glaring at

her. The smiles are gone. It's all business now, and Marv may be a dope with some things, but he's a ruthless shark when he has his business hat on.

Riley stands her ground with her arms crossed. The vein in her neck is getting larger as she goes toe to toe, negotiating with a billionaire. "Five percent," she counters.

"Half a percent," Marv shoots back.

I pull out the calculator on my phone and work out the math. At two million dollars a yacht, she stands to gain six hundred thousand dollars. My mouth drops.

"Deal," she says, shaking his hand.

"Great," Marv says, jumping out of the seat before I can find my voice again. I'm too stunned to talk.

"Marv!" I finally call out as he hurries past Riley. "Wait a second!"

"We already shook on it," he calls out from the hallway as he hurries back to his seat. That mother-fucker!

She's getting over half a million dollars, and all I get is to share a hotel room with her cold ass. She's hot as fuck, but even a week-long sex marathon with her wouldn't be worth six hundred thousand dollars.

She bites her bottom lip as she grins at me. *Maybe it would.*

"Do you hear that, hubby?" she asks with a smug look on her face. "That's the sound of me getting rich."

"The parachute is on that shelf," I say pointing to the wall behind her. "If you still want to use it."

She shakes her head. Her eyes are beaming. "I'm not leaving until I get paid. Then I'll jump out with a parachute made out of one hundred-dollar bills."

*And I'll still be here sitting on my broke ass.*

"Then prepare your waitress station for landing," I say, turning away from her with heat flushing through my body.

"I'm a *flight attendant*," she hisses. "Not a waitress, not a wet t-shirt contest contestant, and not your friend."

I throw her a lazy salute. "Yes, ma'am."

"And when I get my big commission check," she says, clasping her hands together. "I'm going to be a pilot."

Her excitement is starting to piss me off. I didn't think to ask for a commission, but now I'm stuck. Marv would never go back on a handshake.

My lip curls up into a smirk as she starts dancing behind me. That happiness won't last. She's about to be very pissed off when she sees where she's staying.

In *my* room.

# CHAPTER FOUR

## *RILEY*

Mr. Gladstone is yammering in my ear for the forty minutes it takes for the limousine to get from the Cayman Islands airport to our five-star resort. He's not even talking to me. He's on the phone yelling about some shipments that were sent to Yemen instead of Vietnam. *How can someone fuck that up?*

Kara is sitting across from me giving me dirty looks, and Dex is beside her, glancing at my legs every few minutes.

We pull up to our hotel, The Turtle Cove, and I let out a gasp. Apparently, it's the nicest resort in the Cayman Islands, and so far-from the look of the front lobby-it's living up to its reputation. There are towering palm trees swaying in the hot Caribbean breeze, flowers of all sizes, shapes, and colors, and tons of workers running around making it look like a human ant hill.

Two concierge agents meet us with cold glasses of champagne and they're welcoming me to the resort before I even step foot out of the limousine. Traveling rich does have its perks.

I take a sip and moan as the cool bubbles tingle in my mouth and find their way up to my nose.

"Don't spill it," Dex whispers in my ear as he reaches past me for a champagne flute.

I should pour it over his head. I owe him a champagne shower.

Mr. Gladstone bursts out of the limousine and storms up the steps as he yells at the poor sucker on the other end of the line. The concierge agents look at each other in a panic, and then the older-looking one chases after him. Kara follows them both, looking bored as usual.

"My name is Preston, and I'll be your personal concierge," the agent says. "Are you traveling with Mr. and Mrs. Gladstone?"

"We are," Dex answers with a smile. "I'm Mr. Gladstone's personal pilot, and she is his mistress."

Preston's cheeks redden as he looks at me with a look of shock.

"He's kidding of course," I say. "I'm the Captain of the plane and he's my co-pilot. I found him flying moose carcasses up north, and I'm testing him out." I lean in close to Preston and whisper just loud enough for Dex to hear. "I don't think he's going to make it. He doesn't have a steady hand."

A growl rumbles from Dex's throat. "I've yet to show you what I can do with my hands."

"Anyway," I say, straightening up. "I'd love to get to my room."

Preston scans the clipboard in his hands.

"What did you say your name was again?"

"Riley," I say. "Riley Jones."

His face scrunches up like he just smelled a moist gym bag. "I don't have you on the list."

Dex steps in close beside me, and I get a whiff of his rugged cologne mixed with the smell of grease. It's a beautiful combination. "Try, Mr. and Mrs. Dex Jameson," he says, looking at me with a smirk.

*No.*

*Please no.*

Preston smiles and I can feel my reheated lunch creeping back up my throat. "Here you two are. Beachfront. Nice."

*What did I get myself into?*

Dex slides his strong hand around my hip and yanks me close to him. "Don't you remember, baby?" he asks, giving my cheek a fat, wet kiss. "I made the reservations."

He wraps his other hand around my waist and holds me there as I try to squirm away. He's even stronger than he looks.

Dex turns to Preston with a wide grin on his lips. "She'd lose her head if it wasn't attached to her beautiful neck."

"You two seem very in love," Preston says, hugging the clipboard to his chest. It's an odd thing to say considering I'm desperately trying to break free from his grasp, but Preston looks like an odd guy. It's not every day that you meet a man with a pencil-thin mustache.

"We are in love," Dex says, batting his long eyelashes as he stares into my eyes. "We just got married last month. It's our late honeymoon. Isn't that right, honey?"

"Yup," I say shrugging my shoulders. "I was panicking over getting older, and I thought that it was time to settle."

Preston nods. "It's so nice to settle down."

"Not settle down," I say, shaking my head. "Settle for *him*. He's not my number one choice, or even my fifth choice, but his family comes from money, and he's not the worst cook. I just wish he wasn't hung like a five-year-old."

Dex's hands tighten around my waist and he gives me a serious look that makes me start giggling. Preston coughs uncomfortably.

"I didn't hear you complaining last night," Dex says with a hint of annoyance in his voice. I love that I'm getting under his skin. He deserves it. And more.

"I didn't think you would over the sobbing," I say. I turn to Preston and raise an eyebrow. "He always cries during sex. I don't know what it is, but we can never get through a round of sex without him turning on the waterworks."

Preston scratches the side of his cheek and keeps looking around at his colleagues as if he's hoping someone is going to come and save him.

Dex is grinning at me with a look in his eyes that I can't quite place. Admiration maybe?

"Well played," he whispers in my ear before dropping his hands. But I'm not done yet.

A concierge agent is walking by with a bunch of champagne flutes, and I snatch a glass off of his tray. "Honey, look out!" I yell as I throw the champagne into Dex's face. "My goodness, honey," I say, pretending like I'm a concerned wife. "There was a bee on your nose." I turn to Preston as Dex glares at me with champagne pouring down his face onto his pilot's shirt and tie. "He's allergic. That could have gotten ugly."

"Things are about to get ugly," Dex mumbles as he wipes his face with his sleeve.

I fix his tie, brushing my knuckles against his hard upper chest as I lean in close to his ear. "*That* was well played," I whisper, "and I'm just getting started. You don't know who you got into the ring with."

He grins. He's actually enjoying this. But so am I, if I'm being honest.

"I think we're ready to go to our room," I say, turning to Preston. He couldn't look more relieved.

Dex's powerful hand slides down my back and he squeezes my ass with a firm grip. "We sure are! Let's go try out that bed."

I reach behind myself and squeeze my nails into his thick, tattooed forearm until he lets go of my ass. "Please make sure there's extra Kleenex on the nightstand. I don't want my husband's tears getting on the nice bed sheets."

Dex is shaking his head, chuckling to himself as I walk with Preston into the lobby. This hotel is spectacular. Preston points out the many pieces of art displayed between the exotic plants and flowers. He points to an ugly statue of a mermaid who looks like she was sculpted by a blind four-year-old. Her face looks like a stone version of Shrek. "That was given to us by the Japanese President of the Imperial Council after he stayed for two wonderful weeks at our resort."

"It's interesting," I say, grimacing as I stare at her thick nose. "Did he make it himself?"

Preston lets out a squeal of laughter and quickly hides his mouth with his clipboard. "It's not to my tastes either," he whispers, leaning in close.

"Maybe you should throw her back in the ocean," I say, and he laughs again.

"You just got yourself upgraded to the top floor," he says with a grin.

We pass spectacular pool after pool and water fountains that are so beautiful that they should be in an Italian museum. My jaw keeps dropping like I'm a defective marionette.

We finally get to the room and Dex is behind us, keeping a safe distance now that I have recruited Preston to my side and he's outnumbered. Preston hands me the key card and gives me his personal cell phone number, telling me to contact him day or night if we need anything.

"Thanks, Peter," Dex says, wrapping his muscular arms around me once again. My right breast is pressed up against his ribs, and my whole body tingles, responding in an eager way. He kisses me on the neck, sending shivers rushing down my spine as Preston walks away down the hall. I'd be lying if I said that I didn't like it, but I slap his hands away anyway as soon as Preston turns around the corner. Maybe I leave them for an extra second or two.

"Get off of me!" I say, planting my palms on his chest and pushing him away with all my strength. He's like a brick wall and he doesn't move. "Were the kisses really necessary?" I ask as he finally lets go of me.

"As necessary as the glass of champagne in the face," he says, narrowing his eyes at me. "What the hell was that?"

"That was payback," I say, sticking my finger in his face. "Remember that the next time you feel the need to play any of your games with me."

"I didn't realize that you're so competitive," he says. "I love a girl who likes to score."

The way he says everything sounds so sexual. "Ugh," I say, pushing past him into the room.

"Wow," I gasp, looking around. The room is beautiful. Fucking stunning.

The far wall is made up entirely of windows, and the view is pure beach with the gorgeous turquoise ocean spreading out into the horizon. The patio door is open, and the warm breeze and salty ocean air hit my face like a warm kiss. I close my eyes and breathe it in. Not even Dex is going to ruin this moment for me.

"Fuck yeah," he says, walking past me to the hot tub on the balcony. "Why don't you slip out of those sticky clothes and come join me for a test drive?"

"Ugh," I say, rolling my eyes. I underestimated his ability to ruin a moment.

The room is *almost* perfect. I just noticed there's only one bed. The mattress is big enough that we don't have to touch each other, but there's no way I'm sleeping with a jackass like Dex.

I snatch a pillow off the bed and throw it at him. He catches it and looks at me with confusion in his eyes.

"Shotgun the bed," I say. "You can sleep in the hot tub."

He looks at me like I'm crazy. "I'm not sleeping outside."

"Fine," I say, crossing my arms as I stare him

down. "You can sleep in the bathroom."

"We have to play the part, Mrs. Jameson," he says, stepping forward and tossing the pillow back on the bed. "That means sleeping in the same bed."

I roll my eyes at the beautiful man that I'm sharing a bedroom with. The beautiful *arrogant* man. I have to remember that last part, although he's always quick to remind me every time he opens his mouth. "I highly doubt that Prince Kalib will be spying on us throughout the night."

"Who?" he asks, tilting his head to the side.

"You're such an idiot." I grab my beach bag and storm out of the room. It's time to go to the beach and get my mind off of my unwanted roommate.

I change into my bikini in one of the resort's public bathrooms and walk to the beach. The resort is beautiful, but all I can really see is Dex in the back of my mind and the frustratingly hot way that he looks when he smiles.

"Keep your eye on the prize," I mutter to myself as I pass a couple suntanning on beach chairs beside the pool. The man's back is as red as a sunburnt lobster.

*Half a million dollars and change. That's what's on the line.*

My stomach flutters just thinking about it. I've never had a chance at money like this before, and if I'm able to get it all of my dreams will come true. I'll be enrolling in flight school before the ink on the check is dry.

All I have to do is convince the prince that Mr. Gladstone's yachts are the best in the world and fool everyone into thinking that Dex and I are a happily married couple. That last part is the tricky one. We haven't stopped arguing for two seconds since we've met.

I grab a piña colada from the beach bar (gotta love all-inclusive) and walk onto the white sand. It burns my feet, but I love it. There's nothing like the feeling of hot sand spreading between your toes.

The beach is a maze of palm trees and little tiki huts with lazy tourists lying under them, seeking a bit of shade from the hot sun. The turquoise water looks beautiful, and I lie down on an empty beach chair and watch the gentle waves as I take a sip of my drink and then crush a chunk of ice between my teeth that the blender missed.

I can already feel the stress and anxiety that Dex built up in me drifting away on the warm Caribbean breeze. *I can get used to this.*

He really does know how to push all of my buttons. I have to give him that. He had me fuming all day wanting to rip his head off, but for some reason, I can't stop thinking of the way that his hard arms felt wrapped around my body. They felt good. Strong. Sexy.

It's too bad he's the worst. But that may be part of the problem.

I've always been attracted to the bad boy type. That part of my life should have ended with my teenage acne, but I always find myself going back to the same alpha type asshole. Is it bad that I always root for the sexy bad guy in the movies?

His being a pilot isn't helping either. I groan and sink a little lower in my chair as I picture his muscular body hidden by that tight pilot's shirt. I'm not sure if it's the sun or the image of his sleeves rolled up his strong forearms that's making me hot, but I'm ready for a dip in the ocean when I start to wonder what the rest of his body looks like under that shirt.

I'm about to find out because here he comes.

I slink down in my chair and hide behind my fruity drink as Dex walks down the path to the beach. He doesn't see me, thankfully, which means I'm free to stare.

He's jacked, with toned, muscular arms covered in tattoos, a wide chest that screams alpha male, and ripped abs that scream 'touch me.' His black boardshorts are clinging to his hips a little low, just enough to see the carved V plunging into his waistband like an arrow to his cock and just the hint of a shadow of pubic hair.

I gulp.

My pretend husband is fucking hot.

I hate that I'm staring at him, I hate the crude thoughts running through my mind, and I hate that I can't wait for him to walk by me so I can get a glimpse of his ass.

Two hot girls wearing bikinis that must be two sizes too small are walking toward him giggling to each other as they steal glances at him. Anger flashes through me, and I clench my teeth as I watch.

I just know he's going to stop them, and of course, he does. *What a player.*

The angel on my left shoulder is telling me to turn away, but the devil on my right is holding my head in place with his pitchfork.

"Hi," Dex says, flashing them a smile that would have any woman stop dead in her tracks.

And of course, they do. *It's so easy for him.*

The girls' body language says everything. Hands on hips, breasts pressed out, stomachs sucked in, leaning forward. "Take a breath ladies," I whisper. "He's an asshole."

"I've never seen two mermaids *on* the beach," Dex says to them, and they both laugh. The brunette flicks her hair while the blonde slides off her sunglasses and places them on her head to get a better look at him. I can't blame her there.

He has their full attention, and all it took was a cheesy pickup line that never would have worked if he wasn't so goddamned hot. They introduce themselves as Carrie and Nikki as he shakes their hands and openly stares at their perky breasts. They don't seem to mind.

Before I can tell myself that this is a bad idea, I'm getting up and walking over. My commission is on the line, and I can't have that. It's absolutely *not* because I'm jealous. You never know when Prince Kalib could be watching. He could be that old white man who's sleeping on the chair over there. You can never be too careful. Definitely *not* because I'm jealous.

I wrap my arm around Dex's shoulder and he swings his head toward me with a look of shock that quickly turns into a look of defeat. "There you are, honey," I say, tapping my fingers on his warm skin. "I've been looking for you everywhere." I turn to the two girls and smile. "My husband is always wandering around."

Dex is glaring at me, and I give him a little wink.

The girls look disappointed, which makes me happy that I came over here. I lean in close to them.

"He got kicked in the head two years ago by a donkey," I whisper, "and he's never been the same. I think that donkey knocked some screws loose."

The girls look horrified as they take turns glancing from me to Dex. They wish us a good day and hurry away.

"Not cool," Dex says, glaring at me. He looks so hot with the shine of sweat on his toned body. Little specks of sand are clinging to his tanned skin.

"Sorry," I say, raising my nose in the air, "but I don't want my room full of half-naked sluts."

Dex grins. "That's insulting," he says with a frown. "They'd be completely naked sluts."

"Sorry," I say, turning and walking back to my beach chair. "No sluts while we're married. *Honey.*"

"I want a divorce," he calls out.

I turn to him with a smirk. "Let me get paid first."

# CHAPTER FIVE

## *DEX*

"I finish in an hour," Maude says, leaning over on the bar to give me a show. Her low-cut shirt is hanging down, showing off her amazing rack. "Are you still going to be here?"

*Probably not.*

"Yeah, probably," I say as she grabs a maraschino cherry from the bowl in front of her and pops it into her mouth.

"Good," she says with a smile as she crushes the cherry between her perfectly straight teeth. She turns with a bit of a spin, making her amber hair bounce over her sexy shoulders. Maude is one of the bartenders in the lobby bar, and I can see why they put her front and center of the resort. She's got an athletic body with an abundance of curves and a beautiful smile that comes easy and often. She's French Canadian, from Quebec, and she speaks English with the sexiest little accent.

Normally, I'd be all over her, securing the little French tart as my taste for the night, but I can't seem to get into it no matter how many times she bends over in front of me to get beers on the bottom shelf of the fridge.

I glance around the bar past the musicians who are massacring a Bob Marley classic and look for her. I sigh when all I see is empty chairs and a handful of sweaty tourists. *Where is she?*

Riley doesn't strike me as the type to hang out in her room all night watching TV when she's on a beautiful resort like this. I figured she'd be here, or I would have gone to the Sports Bar to watch Thursday Night Football rather than sit here and have my eardrums assaulted by this horrible band.

I check my watch, and it's getting late. Riley would already be here if she was planning on coming to the bar. She's probably curled up in bed dreaming of me.

"Leaving so soon?" Maude asks when I stand up off the barstool. She looks disappointed. She's even hotter when she's pouting, so I'm extra shocked at what I'm about to do.

"Yeah," I say, thanking her for the burger and drinks. I slide a tip across the bar for her. "Maybe we can hang out next time."

She takes the twenty-dollar bill and tucks it into her bra while keeping her stunning eyes locked on me. "We won't be hanging out," she says, with a bite of her bottom lip. "I have better plans than that."

I'm still shaking my head and wondering what the hell is wrong with me as I'm walking through the resort. *Oh, my God. I'm broken.*

It's a sin to have turned down a willing and

ready-to-go girl that hot, and the me from yesterday would have slapped today's me upside the head and ordered me to go back in there. But I'm just not feeling it.

I keep thinking of Riley and wondering what she's up to. *Why do you keep thinking of that stuck-up girl? Yup. You're definitely broken.*

I stop by the Sports Bar to check the score of the football game, and I can't help but smile when I see who is in the middle of a group of rabid Packers fans who are dressed up from their green socks to their cheesehead hats. *They actually packed those?*

Riley cheers and high-fives the Green Bay fans as the Packers defense stops the Lions on third down. She looks adorable wearing a jersey that one of her new friends must have lent her.

I hate the Detroit Lions, but I feel compelled to do it.

"Go Lions!" I yell as I walk into the bar. The table of Detroit fans cheer and bang on the table as they give me the thumbs up and wave me over.

Riley's smile fades to a scowl as her eyes follow me through the bar. I high-five a few of the Lions fans as I sit down at their table, which is next to hers.

A bald guy with a Lions logo on his sweaty cheek pours me a beer from his pitcher. Sweat from the Caribbean heat has melted the face-painted lion into a blue mess. I just hope it didn't drip into the beer.

"Thanks," I say, clinking my beer mug with his. "Party in my room for all of the Lions fans after!" I say, loud enough for Riley to hear.

I can feel the heat from her eyes burning the

back of my head. When I turn around, she's moving her stool, dragging it beside me.

"You're not inviting all of these people to our room," she whispers, her voice racing. "I don't want them there."

I grin. "You want me all to yourself, don't you?"

The table of Packers fans erupts in cheers, and Riley whips her head back around to the large TV. "You made me miss it!" she complains, turning back to me with a glare.

"Don't worry," I say, trying to get under her skin. "Your QB will blow it in the last quarter anyway."

She laughs, sticking her adorable chin in the air. "The only QB that will be choking will be yours."

I lean in nice and close. "The only person who will be choking will be you. Later. On my cock."

"You mean more like gagging on your words."

The table of cheeseheads starts hollering as their wide receiver breaks through the secondary and scores a touchdown.

"Damn it," I curse under my breath. I can't stand losing to her for anything, even in a game where I'm not a fan of either team.

"Choke on this," she says, turning with a wide grin on her luscious lips. She yanks the cheesehead off of her neighbor and slams it onto my head.

"Wooooo!" she screams as she watches her player score on the replay. My table groans as I watch her, cheesehead hat and all, as she stands up on the bar of her stool and gives her new friends high-fives.

"Looks like your party is going to suck," she

says, sitting back down with a grin on her flushed face. "It's going to be full of losers."

"Do I look like a loser?" I ask, wishing that the cheesehead hat wasn't still on my head. "We're only down by three points."

A guy at her table reaches over and plucks his cheesehead hat off of my head. I smooth my hair back in place as Riley laughs at me.

"Three points with only forty seconds left," she says, shaking her head. "Good luck."

The next few minutes are tense as the Lions offense takes the ball up the field. With five seconds left, the clock is stopped with the ball on the twenty-two-yard line. The Lions are out of timeouts, and their kicker is coming on the field about to try and tie the game.

"Here we go," I say, leaning forward. *Why am I actually nervous? I don't even like the Lions.*

"Look at this guy," she says, snorting as she points at the kicker. "He couldn't kick his shoes if they were on his feet."

I've flown fighter jets in combat zones and my heart wasn't pumping as hard as it is now. I rub my hands down the legs of my pants as the kicker lines up and the whistle blows.

The bar is silent as he steps forward and connects with the ball, trying to kick it through the goalposts.

Riley is holding her breath, staring at the screen with wide unblinking eyes. The balls sails through the air and slams into the goalpost with a loud echoing *dong.*

*Damn it.*

Riley and her green and yellow friends

explode into cheers as the clock runs out and the Packers win the game.

"That's what's going to happen every time you try to compete with me," she says, staring at me with a smug look on her face. "You're going to lose."

She doesn't know who she's playing with. I don't lose.

I'm about to tell her that when I feel a tap on my shoulder. "What room is the party in?" someone behind me asks. It's the guy with the sweaty man boobs.

"Four nineteen," I answer, giving him the wrong room.

Riley laughs. "No afterparty?" she whispers, leaning in with a raised eyebrow.

"Not in our room," I whisper back. I don't want these strangers hanging out in my room. I'm still planning on having an afterparty, but only one person is invited. I want Riley all to myself.

"Let's sneak out of here before they follow us," I say, slipping off my stool.

I casually stroll to the bar and then take a quick turn to the exit. Riley is right on my heels. She's still wearing the Packers jersey.

"I didn't peg you for the stealing kind," I say, glancing down at the green and yellow jersey. The thick numbers swallow her perky tits, but she still looks incredible in it. The color really makes her green eyes pop.

"I didn't steal it," she says, thrusting her chin in the air. "It's mine."

I do have to say that I'm impressed. I've never dated a girl who liked football before. Actually, I've never dated anyone long enough to find out.

We walk back to our room, still bickering about the game. I don't really care. I just enjoy getting her all riled up.

"I figured you'd be a fan of the Redskins with the way your cheeks are always blushing around me," I say as I open the door.

I hold it open for her, but she's standing in the hallway, glaring at me with those same cheeks turning red. "And I thought you'd be a Giants fan," she says, crossing her arms. "Because you're a giant dick."

"Come on in," I say, motioning to the doorway with my head, "and we can talk more about my giant dick."

Her jaw clenches shut as her arms fall to her sides. "You and your giant dick can sleep out on the balcony," she says, walking past me with her chin in the air.

My eyes follow her in, dropping down to her ass that's looking amazing in those tight jean shorts. On second thought, it's fitting that she's a Packers fan because she's definitely packing a hot body under there.

It's too bad her personality comes along with it.

"What are you doing?" I ask when I walk into the room. She has one of the many pillows in her hands and is opening the glass door of the balcony.

"Getting your bed ready," she says, tossing the pillow into the hot tub. "Want me to fill it with water for you?"

"Why, so I can drown while sleeping?"

"I didn't think of that," she says with a grin on her face as she turns the water on, soaking my pillow. "Well, that's just a risk we're going to have to take."

I pull off my shirt in one quick movement and toss it onto the desk. "You're the one getting over half a million dollars for this," I say, kicking off my flip flops. "You sleep outside."

She storms back into the room, trying to keep her eyes off of my naked torso. "And what are you getting for this?" she asks, glaring at me. "Shits and giggles? You get to have fun tormenting me?"

*Exactly.* And all of my hard work is working out perfectly.

"So?" she asks, tapping her foot as she waits for my answer. "Why did you agree to this? What's in it for you?"

I look away with a thickness in my throat. If I do this, Riley gets fired, and Kara will thank me in the best possible way.

That's what initially brought me on board, but now it's evolving into something else. I enjoy getting under Riley's skin, and I'm going to enjoy getting under her clothes even more.

"Not everyone blackmails their boss every time that he needs a favor," I say, looking into her narrowed eyes. "I'm doing this because I'm a good employee, unlike you."

She snorts out a laugh. "You?" she says, her shoulders shaking with laughter. "A good employee? You were drinking alcohol while flying an airplane! That not only disqualifies you from being a good employee, it disqualifies you from being a good person."

"Does it disqualify me from getting in your pants?"

She laughs in my face. "The only way you're getting in my pants is if I chop your little pecker off and stuff it into my pocket."

I cringe, taking a reflexive step back from her. Her words still make my stomach drop even though I know she's kidding. Hopefully, she's kidding. That crazed look in her eyes has me wondering.

"You're the one who blackmailed Marv," I say, raising my chin as I stare down at her. "Does that make you a good person?"

"I'm getting money from my boss to do a job," she says, glaring up at me. "That's what bosses do. They give their employees money."

"Especially when they get blackmailed by them."

She swallows hard as she glares at me. "Oh look," she says, turning to the open doors on the balcony. "Your bed-slash-bath is ready. I put it on freezing cold so your cold-blooded body can feel right at home."

I slip off my shorts as she walks out and turns off the water. Her eyes widen and she freezes in the doorway when she sees my tight gray boxer briefs. She subtly shakes her head and looks away, but I can see that she's breathing faster. Her skin is flushing that adorable pink as she suddenly takes an interest in the hotel pamphlet on the nightstand.

Her eyes dart to me as I walk to the side of the bed and pull back the sheets. "I'm not sleeping outside," I say, slipping under the covers. "And I'm not sleeping on the floor, or in the bathroom, or in the hallway. I'm sleeping with you."

I wonder what's softer, the sheets on the bed or the skin that's hiding under Riley's green and yellow jersey? I hope I'm about to find out.

"I'd never sleep with you," she says, glaring at me with disgust. She yanks one of the pillows off of the bed and stomps to the balcony door. "I'd rather sleep outside than be in your arrogant, cocky, vain, asshole presence for a second longer."

"You'd rather sleep with the Caribbean insects?" I ask, leaning up on my elbow. She stops at the door but doesn't turn, listening to me with her eyes trained on the square tiles. I've got her now. "Have fun with the giant mosquitoes, stinging hornets, deadly scorpions, snapping fire ants, and nasty spiders."

"Spiders?" she whispers, cringing as she looks at me.

"Oh yeah," I say, nodding. "Big hairy ones. They shouldn't bother you too much," I say, trying to hide my grin. "They only come out around the time the sun rises. Just tie your hair back in a ponytail because they like to crawl into open hair and lay their eggs."

She shudders as she slams the door closed.

"Fine," she says, throwing the pillow back onto the bed.

I give her a triumphant grin as I tap the sheets beside me.

"Spiders are the one thing that's creepier than you," she says, stomping across the room toward her luggage. "But not by much."

I watch her curiously as she grabs her large bulky suitcase and slams it in the middle of the bed. It bounces on the mattress beside me. She's all flared nostrils and angry grunts as she picks up my suitcase and throws it down behind hers, completing the barrier of cheap luggage. The great wall of made in China.

"That's better," she says, huffing out a breath as she storms back to her side of the bed. "No touching."

"I couldn't if I tried," I say, staring at her huge suitcase wall. "You should go work with Donald Trump. He could use your wall building skills."

The bed bounces slightly as she gets in. My view is blocked by a Samsonite logo.

"If I can use my position to get you deported," she says, "then I'll sign up first thing tomorrow morning."

I shift in the bed, raising my head over the suitcase for a second to see her lying between the sheets. She still has her shorts and jersey on. She's either a really dedicated fan or she really hates me.

I'm not sure if I want to know the answer to that one.

"Goodnight, wifey," I say in a singsong voice.

"Don't call me that," she says with a shudder in her voice. "You're going to give me nightmares."

I smile as I tuck my arm under my pillow and rest my head down. She thinks she's in a nightmare now. Wait until she meets the prince and has to pretend to be my adoring wife.

I'm going to make her earn every penny of that commission.

Then, she'll know what a true nightmare is.

# CHAPTER SIX

## *RILEY*

I groan when I wake up to someone pounding on the outside of the door.

"Go away!" Dex yells to the maids. "Sleeping!"

For once, he says something that I agree with. It's still dark out.

I turn over, rubbing my eyes, and come face to face with my handy makeshift wall of suitcases. It's still between us, separating the two sides of the bed like heaven and hell. I'll let you guess which side has the devil on it.

"Open up," a muffled voice calls through the door. The voice is a little deep for a maid.

"Shit," Dex mumbles as he gets out of bed. I peek over the luggage wall like a soldier taking a look over the parapet of a castle to see the enemy. The enemy is in boxer briefs. The enemy is armed with sexy tattoos and a nice ass. The enemy will be the death of me if I'm not careful.

Dex takes a deep breath before opening the door. Marv is there, bursting in like a cannonball. He's fully dressed and showered, looking *way* too awake considering the sun isn't out yet.

Dex turns to me as he yawns. "Did you order a billionaire?"

I sit up in bed, giving Marv a wide smile even though I'm cursing him in my head. "Good morning, Mr. Gladstone," I say, trying to sound chipper despite my groggy voice. "Up nice and early I see."

"I'm up at four a.m. every morning," he says, pounding his chest with a fist. "It's the billionaire way."

I'd rather keep my broke ass little bank account and sleep in until noon, but that's not what I tell him.

"I love getting up before the sunrise," I lie as I jump out of bed and open the curtains. There's no sunlight to let in.

"Oh, God," Dex says, rubbing his eye as he stumbles back to the bed. "I'm the only sane one here."

He belly flops onto the bed with a sigh as Marv closes the door.

"We have a busy day," Marv says, charging into the room like a seasoned general. He tilts his head as he looks at the suitcase wall down the middle of the bed but doesn't say anything about it. "We're meeting Prince Kalib today."

"Great," I say, grinning. The faster I meet the prince, the faster I can charm him into buying sixty yachts, the faster I get my money, the faster I can quit, and the faster I can go to flight school to become a pilot.

"Are we meeting him for breakfast?" Dex asks with his face smushed into the pillow. "Does the prince get up at ungodly hours as well?"

"We're meeting him for lunch," Marv says with a smile. "On his private island."

"Private island?" Dex asks, finally looking awake. "Are we taking the jet?"

"Nope," Marv says, shaking his head. "There's no runway. The concierge is getting us a float plane."

"Are they getting us a responsible pilot as well?" I mumble.

They both turn and narrow their eyes at me. "I mean, what time are we leaving?"

"I want to see both of you in the lobby at nine," Marv says. He glances at the suitcases on the bed and he takes a deep breath. "Are you two going to be able to play nice?"

"Yes," we both say, not looking at each other.

"I want happily married couple," he says, looking from me to Dex like a principal who's warning two unruly students. "Not an 'about to get divorced' married couple, and not an 'I married him for the money but secretly hate him married couple.' Can you two pull that off?"

We glance at each other and nod. Dex's hair is all messy from sleeping, but somehow, he looks even hotter. It's not fair. My hair is plastered to the sides of my head like I slept in a motorcycle helmet.

"There's a lot of money on the line," Marv says, his voice tense and serious. He doesn't have to remind me about that. There's six hundred thousand dollars on the line for me, and I'm not about to let some stupid rivalry between me and Captain Fuck Face get in the way of that.

"I won't let you down," I say, standing up straight. "You can count on me."

Marv stares at me for a second and then sighs. "What about you?" he asks Dex. "Can you play nice?"

"I'll be my regular charming self," Dex says while scratching his balls over his boxer briefs.

"That's what I'm afraid of," Marv answers with a sigh. He furrows his brow when he sees the hot tub full of water with the pillow floating on the surface. "I don't want to know."

"She did it," Dex says, pointing at me. "She tried to seduce me, but I turned her down. I'm trying to stay professional."

"You're the one walking around in your underwear!" I snap back.

"You're the one who keeps looking," he answers.

"Stop!" Marv shouts, shutting us both up. "I'm selling sixty yachts today. If I don't, it's coming out of your paychecks."

Dex laughs. "That would take me a hundred lifetimes to pay off with what you pay me."

"Then act professional," he snaps. "Otherwise you'll be flying around the devil in the afterlife to pay your debt."

"I'm already flying around with the devil," I say, glaring at Dex. "And I can tell you that it sucks."

It's only five a.m. and Marv already looks like he's in desperate need of a stress ball.

He rubs his forehead as he walks to the door. "Nine a.m. in the lobby," he says as he opens it. He glances down at his Rolex and takes a deep breath.

"You two have four hours. I suggest you get your story straight."

"Story straight?" Dex repeats.

"You two are supposed to be married," he says, looking as frustrated as a dateless virgin on prom night. "You should know information about each other."

"Will do, boss," I say, nodding at him. "You can count on us."

Marv stares at me for a moment and then lets out another sigh. He steps out of the room and closes the door without saying another word.

"We should know everything about each other," Dex says, turning onto his back. It takes everything I have not to glance down at his chiseled abs.

I hate to admit it but he's right. One little slip up can cause all of this to come crashing down. If I don't know how he takes his coffee or if we contradict each other about where we live, our last name, our jobs, anything, Prince Kalib will know there's something up.

He grins as he leans up on his elbow, watching me over the suitcases. "We should know what our spouse looks like naked," he says. "You can go first."

If my eyes could shoot laser beams, his head would be in the shape of a canoe.

"What's to know?" I ask, glaring at him. "I'm hot as shit, and if anyone asks, you have a three-inch dick. There. Settled."

He chuckles as he drops his head back onto the pillow, smiling as he stares up at the ceiling. I finally get a chance to glance at his abs, and I can tell you that he sure as shit didn't skip ab day.

"I always thought my wife would be nice," he says, rubbing his bearded chin.

"Shitty husbands make shitty wives," I say as I pick up his shirt and throw it at him.

"So, everything is my fault?" he asks, looking at me in disbelief.

I give him my fakest smile. "Sure is! Welcome to married life, hubby."

"You have the most beautiful smile," Dex says, making me cringe.

He's not talking to me. He's talking to the young blonde waitress at the restaurant where we're eating breakfast.

She glances at my left hand quickly and then smiles at him when she doesn't see a ring on my finger. *That reminds me...*

"Thank you," she says, tilting her head as she leans on the table, staring at him like he's a famous celebrity and she's trying to get invited back to his trailer.

"What's your name?" he asks, leaning toward her. He's trying to make me jealous. That's all this is. But the jokes on him because it's not working.

She thrusts her chest out, sticking her perky breast absurdly close to his face. "Sofia," she says, showing him more than just her name tag.

Dex takes much longer than necessary to read one word. Or maybe he has the reading ability of a kindergartner. I wouldn't be surprised.

I grab my paper napkin and tear it into a million pieces under the table as I watch the two of them flirt. Definitely *not* jealous.

"Such a pretty name," he says, flashing his straight white teeth at her. She's slutty putty in his hands. "Isn't Sofia such a pretty name?" he asks, turning to me with a grin.

"Mm-hm," I mutter through my clenched jaw. "I like how it rhymes with gonorrhea."

Sofia shoots me a dirty look before turning back to Dex with a soft smile. "What's your name?" she asks him.

"It also rhymes with diarrhea," I interrupt, "and North Korea." Okay, that last one was a stretch.

"My name is Dex," he says, rubbing his arrogant chin as he ogles her. "And this is my assistant, Riley."

"Co-worker," I correct.

Sofia doesn't seem to care. She's not nearly as interested in me.

*Time to pour some ice on this fire before it gets out of control and I'm sleeping in the hallway.*

"Co-worker slash wife," I say, trying to stifle my laugh at Gonorrhea's shocked face. "Can we order now, please? My husband gets very cranky when he doesn't eat."

Gonorrhea backs away from the table and pulls out her notepad, giving me a glassy stare as I open the menu. "You go ahead, honey."

Dex sighs in defeat, slumping down in the booth as Sofia stares down at the table. Is it bad that I'm loving the awkwardness?

"I'll just take the bacon and eggs," he says, handing her the menu as he lets out a long, low sigh.

"Eggs?" I say, lowering my menu as I stare at him with feigned concern. "Are you sure it's a good idea to eat that, honey?"

He's staring at me with an icy glare. "Why wouldn't it be? Honey."

I have to hold in my laugh as I pretend to be the concerned wife. "Your IBS will kick in." I lean in close to Gonorrhea and lower my voice. "He has irritable bowel syndrome. Just one bite of an egg and his asshole will turn into a fire hose for the rest of the day. It's disgusting, but I still love him, even though he does cost us a fortune in toilet paper."

The tip of his lips curls up into a half smile as I reach across the table and take his hand in mine. "It's a challenge for both of us," I say, nodding as I look at him with soft eyes. "And we have to replace our toilet at least once a year, but our love is worth the struggle."

"Are you finished?" he whispers to me.

I shake my head slowly. "I'm just getting started."

He gulps as he turns to the waitress, not looking nearly as confident as before. "Just bring us some pancakes please."

Gonorrhea looks at me and I nod. It was what I was going to order anyway.

She hurries away from our table like his made-up IBS is contagious.

"Irritable bowel syndrome?" he asks, shaking his head as he watches me. "Really?"

"I improvised," I say, grinning. "You always have shit spewing out of your mouth, so I thought it was fitting."

He leans back in the booth and laughs. "You

were just jealous."

"Ha!" I scream, a little too loud. Way too loud, actually. People at the neighboring tables lower their waffle and egg covered forks to turn and look at me. "We're supposed to give the appearance that we're married. How is it going to look if you're getting numbers from slutty waitresses?"

He rolls his eyes as he grabs his empty coffee cup and looks in it. "We could have had great service because of me, but she's probably hiding in the back now because of you."

*And I couldn't be happier.*

"Let's get down to work," I say, folding my hands on the table as I put on my business face. "We have to know the basics about each other."

"Fine," he says, running his hand through his hair. The short sleeve of his t-shirt falls down his arm, showing off a tattooed tricep. I swallow the whimper that's crawling up my throat.

"What's your favorite position?" he asks.

"For what?"

He leans in with a raised eyebrow. "For when we're together."

I take a deep breath as I glare at his frustratingly beautiful face. "My favorite position for when we're together is me turned away from you with my hands over my ears."

He grabs my pen and scribbles on his napkin as he nods his head. "So, doggystyle. Nice. I was picturing you on top, but this is good too."

"I'm picturing you with your head in a vise," I say in a tight voice.

He just ignores me, tapping the pen on his strong chin. "So, doggystyle. Facing a mirror?"

"Ha!" I laugh, crossing my arms and leaning back as I stare at him in disbelief. "You are so in love with yourself. Of course, you would have to be facing a mirror when you have sex. Would I have to put on your cologne as well, so you can close your eyes and pretend that you're having sex with yourself?"

"No," he says, shaking his head as he grins at me. "I like your smell. It smells like pent-up sexual aggression mixed with denial."

I huff out another laugh. The pent-up sexual aggression I'll give him, but the denial? No.

"Denial of what?"

He leans over the table and holds my eyes with his icy blues. My heart starts pounding in my chest as the hair raises on my arms. *Why does he have to be so hot? This would be so much easier if his face matched the ugliness of his soul.*

"Denial that you want me to pick you up, throw you over my shoulder, bring you to our room, and not let you out until your legs are trembling, you're covered in sweat, and everyone in the resort knows my name."

The sexy timbre of his voice sends warm shivers through my body which mix with the flood of warmth brought on by his words. I hold my breath, barely able to breathe under his intense stare.

My palms are so sweaty that I'm wishing I didn't make confetti out of my napkin.

"You're the one in denial," I say, swallowing the increased saliva in my mouth.

"This should be good," he says, raising his chin as he waits for it. "What am I in denial of?"

"That I'm not attracted to you," I say, trying not to scratch my cheek, look away, or do any of the other poker tells that will show I'm lying. "That not every woman on the planet wants to see you naked or have disappointing sex with you."

The waitress interrupts us when she returns to the table with a pot of coffee. She fills our cups in record time and hurries away before either of us can talk to her.

Dex stares at me as he opens a milk and pours it into his coffee. "So, one milk," I say, taking my pen back and writing it on the pad of paper that I brought. "We should know how we take each other's coffee. I take mine with *two* milks."

He doesn't write it down. Why is he not writing it down?

"Where do we live?" I ask, tapping my chin with the pen.

"Colorado."

"Why would we need a yacht if we live in Colorado?"

"Fine," he says, rolling his eyes. "Miami."

I think about it for a second and then nod. "That's good." I write it in the notes.

"Do we have any pets?" I ask.

He takes a sip of his coffee and grins. "Why don't you tell me?"

"Two dogs," I say, writing it down. "Sherry is our German Shepherd, and Canuck is our pug. We rescued him while on vacation in Canada."

"We rescued him?" he asks, raising an eyebrow. "From a fire or something?"

"No," I say, frowning at him. "From the pound."

"Okay, Wonder Woman," he says, laughing at me. "You walked into the pound and rescued him.

You're such a hero."

"Fine," I say, aggressively crossing out the last line with my pen. "No pets. What do you do for a living?"

He hums as he thinks about it. "Elementary school teacher."

I jerk my head back in surprise. With his huge frame and hard round muscles covered in ink, an elementary school teacher is the last thing that he looks like. He turns away, looking embarrassed as I stare at him, trying to figure it all out.

"What?" he asks with a shrug. "I like kids."

"Do you know any elementary school teachers who own a yacht?"

He sighs. "Why don't you just tell me what I do for a living? What do I look like to you?"

*A model, a rockstar, a pornstar, the Devil.*

"Let's go with real estate investor."

"And you were a mail order bride," he says before casually taking a sip of his coffee.

"What?"

"I picked you out of a catalog."

"What is wrong with you?" I ask, furrowing my brow. "I'm a smart, independent, working woman."

He just shrugs.

We go on like this, hammering out details until our pancakes arrive. At least, I go on like this. Dex sits there, looking more bored by the minute.

He's still not writing any of it down.

His continued lack of giving any fucks is starting to get on my nerves.

We eat fast so we can grab our bags and head to the lobby in time. He doesn't seem to be listening as I reread him my notes, trying to slam the information into his thick skull.

"All right," Marv says when we see him in the lobby. "From this point forward, you two are happily married owners of a yacht."

Dex is grinning as he looks down at me. "By the power vested in me, I now pronounce you the luckiest woman in the world."

"Great," I say, glaring back at him. "You may now kiss my ass."

# CHAPTER SEVEN

*RILEY*

I'm giddy with anticipation as I walk down the dock to the plane that's floating in the turquoise ocean. It's a Cessna 185 fitted with floating pontoons that will let us take-off and land in water. I've never been in a float plane before even though it's been on my bucket list since I was six-years-old.

Dex slaps the ass of the plane that's bouncing up and down in the water and grins at me. "I like my girls bouncy and wet before I slip inside of them."

My bucket list is quickly turning into a fuck-it list. All I want to do is fill the bucket with wine when I'm around this guy.

He opens the door of the four-seater plane and slips inside without doing the necessary outside checks.

"Excuse me," I say, knocking on his window as I stand on the dock. "You didn't do the walk-around!"

He sighs before opening the window and looks at me as he slides his Ray Ban aviator sunglasses on. *Fuck, he looks hot in those.* I think about taking a quick dip in the ocean to cool off before getting inside.

"What?" he asks, huffing out a breath.

"You didn't do the walk-around," I say, staring at my reflection in his mirrored sunglasses. *Do I really look that uptight?*

"The plane is floating in water," he says, dipping his sunglasses down so he can see me uninterrupted. "I don't do swim-arounds."

Thankfully, Marv and Kara are walking up the dock behind me. Marv is pounding something onto his phone with his thick fingers as Kara scowls at me. She has the beauty of a mermaid with the personality of a pirate. I just wish I could strand her out to sea where she belongs.

"Mr. Gladstone," I say in my high pitched someone's-not-following-the-rules voice. "I regret to inform you that Dex hasn't performed all of the necessary checks before starting the airplane."

He barrels past me. "And I regret to inform you that I don't care." He rips open the back door of the plane as he stuffs his phone into his pocket. "Can you swim?"

"Yes," I say meekly as Kara flashes me a dirty look while she struts past me.

"Then don't worry so much," Marv says as he gets in the plane. "Dex is a skilled pilot."

"Why are you so afraid of dying?" Kara asks, grinning at me behind her designer sunglasses. "It's not like anyone is going to be that upset if you do. Lighten up."

My hands are clenched into fists as I grind my teeth, watching her climb into the backseat after Marv. She grins at me as she shuts the door.

The engine sputters as Dex starts the plane. I'm still seething at Kara's words as the propeller on the nose of the plane starts spinning, sending my brown hair flying into my face.

*If he's not going to do the walk-around, then I will.*

He's grinning at me through the window as I carefully look the plane up and down, running my fingertips over every bolt to make sure they're nice and tight. I run my hands over the flaps to make sure they're not obstructed by anything like a bird who decided to nest in there. The pilot's side of the aircraft is parked against the dock but there's no way I can get to the other side without a bathing suit.

Dex pops his head out of the window with a shit-eating grin on his face. "What about the other side of the airplane?"

"Shut up," I say, looking away from his smug face.

He doesn't shut up. He just rubs it in deeper. "Performing a walk-around is an FAA regulation," he says in an official-sounding voice. "Better get your arm floaties on."

I fold my arms across my chest as I turn away, avoiding having to look at the frustrating pilot. "Fine," I say in a sharp tone. "Let me in."

Dex opens his door and grins. He looks gorgeous with his thick, toned legs sticking out of his shorts, his inked-up muscular arms, the aviator sunglasses, and headset resting around his neck. His wicked mouth is grinning at me, making my insides turn as fast as the propeller. He's just my type-until he opens his goddamn mouth.

"Climb over," he says, patting his lap.

"No!" I say, trying to melt him with my stare. "You get out first."

He shrugs with a knowing smile on his lips. "You know as well as I do that once the engine is running, the pilot is forbidden to leave the Captain's seat."

"Since when do you follow the rules?"

He bites his bottom lip as he looks me up and down. "Since it benefits me."

I take a deep breath as I look around, wondering what to do. He'll just refuse to get out, but I don't want to crawl over him like he's about to give me a spanking.

Marv makes my decision easier. "Get in the plane or you can walk back to LA!" he yells, sticking his big head between the seats.

This goes against everything I stand for, but I really need that money, so I swallow my pride and climb up. Dex smiles, laughing at me as I place my hand on his hard thigh and crawl over him. There's not a lot of room between him and the yoke, so my body crushes against his as I hurry over.

He tries to help me over by putting a hand on my ass so I slam a knee into his groin as a thank you.

"Oompf," he grunts, swallowing hard as I crawl into the passenger's seat with my heart racing. "I always knew you were a ball buster but *fuck*."

"Good to see you two looking like a married couple," Marv says, sticking his head between us. "With all of the fighting up there, it feels like I'm a kid again watching my parents on a road trip. But we agreed on *happy couple*, not miserable-I-made-amistake-in-marrying-you couple."

"You're asking for an Oscar performance," I mumble. Do I look like Meryl Streep?

Dex slips on his headset, and I slip on mine as well. It's loud in the plane with the engine on, and the headsets allow the pilot to speak with the air traffic controllers watching over the airspace, and it also allows everyone inside the plane to talk to each other.

Marv doesn't bother putting his set on. He's too interested in his phone, and Kara has her iPhone buds in her ears.

I have no interest in speaking with Dex after what he just pulled, but I want to make sure he doesn't mess anything up with the air traffic controllers, so I put mine on. I have to keep this mongrel on a short leash.

"Where are the maps?" I ask through the microphone when I don't see them anywhere.

Dex pulls out his phone and thumbs through it. "In here." His deep voice crackles in my ear.

"The physical maps," I say, holding my breath as I wait for his answer, which I'm sure I'm not going to like.

"I don't use any of that shit," he says, opening an app. "I have a GPS on here."

I grind my teeth as I try to control my anger. The Global Navigation Satellite System is a very practical and useful tool, but it's not sufficient in navigating an aircraft. The GPS, or Global Positioning System, is owned and operated by the US Government. They make it freely available to anyone with a GPS receiver, but they can shut it down at any time, which they've done once to the Indian military in 1999 during the Kargil War. Physical maps must be onboard the aircraft.

"What if your phone dies or the GPS system is shut off?" I ask, waving my hands around as I talk. "What if the app fails or a storm system interrupts our—"

Something gets interrupted all right, but it's not our navigational system, it's me. Dex shuts off my microphone. The switch is on the left side of the instrument panel. It's out of my reach.

*Whatever. It's not like he was listening to me anyway.*

A worker jogs over and unties the rope that's keeping us secured to the dock. He pushes the plane away and waves as we bounce up and down on our way toward the open water.

My eyes are locked on Dex's hands as he flicks switches and pushes buttons. I've done this a million times on my flight simulator game, and even though Dex seems like he wouldn't be able to fly a kite in a hurricane, he doesn't miss a step.

"Welcome aboard, Dex Airlines," he says as the plane picks up speed. He looks down at my legs and grins. "Where our passengers always *come* first." He drawls out the word come, making the tiny hairs on my arms raise.

It's weird hearing him through the headset. It's like he's in my head, penetrating my thoughts, taking over my brain, invading my mind. I couldn't get him out of my head this morning, but this is much worse. It's physical now.

My heart starts hammering in my chest as the plane shoots across the flat water like a rocket. Dex is distracted with the take-off, so I lean back and carefully look at him with a sideways glance.

He's such a cocky asshole, but watching him

so relaxed and in control as he pilots the plane, slowly lowering the yoke until the pontoons leave the water, has me breathless. He does it with such ease, such grace.

He's in total control the entire time, and it's making my body tremble.

"Control yourself, Riley," I whisper to myself as the plane flies off the water and climbs through the sky. *Don't get distracted by this guy. Just get your money and run.*

Dex is flying me into the sky now, but if I'm not careful, he's going to take me crashing down with him.

An hour and a half later, we're circling the most spectacular island that I've ever seen. In between the cover of a tropical forest is an enormous villa that snakes across the private island. I count seven white sand beaches around the island, nine inground swimming pools, and only four people.

With all of the yachts and jet skis parked on the beach, the helicopter on the roof, and the numerous tennis courts, it looks like a Disney World for adults.

I'm shocked, really. I don't know what I was expecting from a man about to buy sixty yachts, but this is incredible. It's hard to imagine that one person can have so much wealth when all I have to compare is my mom's little two-bedroom apartment that I grew up in.

"Whoa," Dex says as he looks down at the island. "This guy makes you look like you're on food stamps, Marv."

Marv and Kara had put on the headsets about ten minutes ago when Dex announced that we were close. He also flicked my microphone back on with a warning that he would turn it off if I doubted his genius one more time.

He didn't say anything against giving him the finger, so I did that instead.

Marv snorts out a laugh from the back seat. "Please," he says through the headsets. "That's all royalty money. I clawed my way up from the inner city."

"Yeah," Kara says, the annoyance clear in her voice. "The inner city of Bel Air."

My hands are glued to the window as I stare down at the island. "Oh, my gosh!" My mouth flies open when I see a crazy fuck surfing in the tsunami-sized waves on the north side of the island. He looks like an ant who's getting flushed down the toilet but is somehow still in control as he surfs the crests of the waves.

"That must be the prince," Marv says, chuckling as he watches. "I heard he's quite the surfer."

That's an understatement. He stands up tall on his board when he spots us and waves. I can't look. He's on the crest of a liquid skyscraper, and he's waving to us like any wrong move won't mean his immediate death and the immediate death of my six hundred thousand dollars.

Dex dips the wing of the plane, an aerial wave

back to him, and circles around to the south side of the island to land on the smooth water.

Again, I'm on full alert as I watch Dex's every move on the way down. I hate to admit it, but he is a skilled pilot. He lands the plane as softly as a leaf landing on a lake in autumn.

He turns to grin at me, but I'm not about to give him any satisfaction. I turn away, marveling at the mini mall-sized villa as Dex steers the plane toward the beach.

The villa staff rushes out of the front door as Dex beaches our plane on the white sand. As soon as the engine is off, Marv grabs me and Dex by the arms. He gives our arms a hard squeeze to let us know he's serious.

"If you two fuck this up for me with your bickering," he says, his tight voice making me gulp, "I will use all of my wealth and influence to destroy you, your future kids, your future grandkids, even your fucking pets. Got that?"

We both gulp out a 'yes sir' at the same time.

"I mean it," he warns. "Even the birds and squirrels living in your backyards will be drowned in debt and litigation when I'm done with you two."

Marv storms out of the plane and I quickly follow. "Sir," I say, giving him my best smile. "I promise I will do everything I can to make this deal go through."

"Everything?" he asks, raising his eyebrow. "With Prince Kalib, your faithfulness to the company may be tested."

"What do you mean?" I ask, taking a worried step back.

He shrugs as he takes off toward the villa,

kicking up the white powdery sand as he goes. "Don't worry. You'll be fine. Probably."

I'm wanting to crawl back into the plane and hide under the seat when Kara taps me on the shoulder.

"Yes, Mrs. Gladstone?" I say. My smile is so tight that I'm worried my lips are going to snap.

"What did I tell you about flirting with my husband?" she asks, flexing her CrossFit arms as she folds them across her chest.

"Not to do it," I say in a flat voice. "And I still haven't."

She reaches out, grabs my nipple, and squeezes it hard, turning her hand until I scream out in pain.

"I don't like you," she hisses before spinning on her heels and marching up the sand, trying to stay upright in her long heels.

*What is wrong with these people?*

It's like I'm stranded on an island with no escape. Like I'm on Jurassic Park, but instead of man-eating dinosaurs, I'm trapped with way more vicious beasts.

"Ready?" Dex asks, grinning as he holds out his arm. "Wifey."

I glance over at the rainforest, hoping for a T-Rex to come rushing out and end this torture quickly, but I'm not that lucky.

So, I go with the caveman instead.

# CHAPTER EIGHT

## *DEX*

"Dex!"

It's Kara. She wants something. I can tell by the way her tits are thrust up in the air.

"Go on ahead," I say to the feisty girl on my arm. "I'll be up there in a minute."

"Take your time," Riley mutters as she unhooks her arm from mine and walks up the sand. I take a second to admire her perfectly round ass before I turn back to Kara.

She's trying to smile sweetly at me, but I can smell the venom boiling behind those luscious lips. "What is she still doing here?"

Kara is leaning against a palm tree, looking pissed as usual. She's so hot when she's mad. She's so hot all of the time.

"The big man needs her," I say, shrugging as she bites her bottom lip. "We have to pretend to be husband and wife for the prince. He wants us to act like we're happy owners of one of his yachts." It sounds like a stupid idea to me, but when it comes to business, Marv always knows what he's doing.

"Can I be your mistress?" she asks, tucking a finger between her tanned shoulder and pink bra strap. Her pouty lips part as she gives me some killer fuck-me eyes.

"Of course," I say, stepping in with my hands out, reaching for her. She spins away before I can touch her.

"Get rid of *her* first," she says, kicking up white sand as she skips away. "And then I'm all *yours*."

I can't help but laugh as she jogs up the beach. This chick wrote the book on teasing cock.

I've been dreaming about her for years, and now I'm so close. All I have to do is help Marv get these yachts sold and she's all mine.

I walk up the beach, admiring the view as I go. I've seen a lot of stunning places while working for Marv, but this one is definitely at the top of the list. Marv's private jet could fit in the lobby of the villa. It's not like the prince needs it. He's got an Augusta Westland AW101 helicopter parked on the roof. It's basically the Lamborghini of helicopters.

*I wonder if he needs a pilot? I'll probably be looking for a job after I nail the boss's wife.*

My three passengers are already talking to the prince by the pool. He's dripping wet in only a bathing suit and has a surfboard tucked under his arm.

He's got his eyes fixated on Riley.

My stomach hardens when she laughs at his words, and I move a little faster, clenching my teeth as I go.

"I wasn't expecting such beauties," he says, glancing at Kara quickly and then turning to openly stare at Riley once again. Her cheeks redden as she smiles shyly at him. "You remind me of a girl that I fell in love with when I went to school in America."

Anger surges through me as I picture grabbing his surfboard and breaking it over his pretty boy head. He's a good-looking man with olive skin and a short cropped beard. He's fit with an athletic body and a smile that I can tell the girls would like.

I step beside Riley and wrap my arm around her shoulder possessively before she gets any ideas.

"Hello," I say, glaring at him in a challenging way. "I'm Riley's *husband*, Dex."

He smiles easily at me as he reaches out to shake my hand. I give him a firm grip just in case he doesn't realize who the real alpha male is. These two guys may have bigger bank accounts and own more toys than me, but I've got the real stuff. I'm the real alpha wolf here.

"Good afternoon, Dex," he says with only the slightest accent. "I was just saying how beautiful your wife is."

"She is a looker," I say, wrapping a hand around her waist and yanking her in close. I have to stifle a laugh when she puts a palm on my chest and tries to push me away.

"Honey," she says, staring up at me with tight eyes. "We're guests here. Let's not act inappropriately."

"Nonsense," Prince Kalib says, waving his hand at her. "We're in paradise, and this is a palace of love. Your body is a masterpiece and deserves to be treated as such."

"That's right, honey," I say, grinning as I slide a hand over her gorgeous ass. "Your body is a masterpiece. Your tight ass should be in a museum."

She smiles at me, but there's fire brimming behind her eyes. "Your ass is going to be in a *mausoleum* if you don't get your hands off of me," she hisses through clenched teeth.

"Your breasts are magnificent," Prince Creep says, openly staring at her chest. "Are they real?"

Riley turns, looking like she's about to slap him, but I hold her back. This opportunity is too good to waste.

"Let me answer this one, honey," I say, smiling at her. She finally relaxes after the shock of the question has worn off. "They are real," I say, nodding at the prince. I gently cup the bottoms of her tits as she glares at me. "They are so soft and supple, yet firm and perky at the same time."

She gives me a look that lets me know I'm going to pay for every tap, squeeze, and caress later. I don't care. Right now, this feels fucking amazing. I just wish I didn't have an audience staring at us.

"Can I touch?" the prince asks, stepping forward.

To my surprise, Riley turns to me and grins. "I'll let my husband decide that."

A low growl escapes my throat as I turn to him. "Don't touch my wife," I hiss through clenched teeth. The way he's reaching for her is making my nostrils flare.

It's not like I'm jealous over a stuck-up girl like Riley, but for some reason the thought of another man's hands on her is stirring me into a murderous rage.

Marv is quick to diffuse the mood by pulling the prince away. "So, Prince Kalib," he says, slipping his arm over the prince's shoulder as he guides him back to the villa. "I hear you need some yachts." His voice trails as they walk away. Kara follows behind them, looking bored as usual.

Riley spins, baring her teeth at me when we're alone. "What. The. Hell. Was. That?" she demands, her legs planted wide, and her hands squeezed into fists.

"Just playing the part," I shrug, feigning innocence.

She crosses her arms as her lips flatten into a straight line, her heated eyes making me wish that I wore SPF 1000 sunblock. "Groping your wife in public is playing the part?"

I can't help but grin. "If you were my wife, I would grope you at every chance that I got."

Her shoulders loosen as she exhales long and hard. "I can believe that," she says, biting her bottom lip as she stares at me. "No more touching my breasts. Or my ass. Or anything on me, really. You stay just out of arm's length."

"Six hundred thousand dollars," I say, reminding her of what's on the line. "I thought you wanted to enroll in flight school."

"I do," she says, sighing as her arms fall to her sides. "But I don't want to prostitute myself to get there."

"It's not prostitution if you like it," I say, raising an eyebrow.

"I don't."

"Are you sure," I ask, grinning at her. "I could have sworn I felt your heart beating harder."

"It was," she says, swallowing hard. "From anger."

"I have to touch you one more time," I say, digging into my pocket.

"That better be a gun that you can put to my head," she says, watching my hand with a guarded look. "Because that's the only way I'm letting you touch me again."

Her face tells a different story when she sees what I have: two diamond rings.

"What's that?" she asks, her eyes transfixed on the huge diamonds.

"You don't think I'd let my wife walk around without some bling on her ring finger, do you?"

Her sexy lips part as I gently take her left hand and slide the rings on. "Just don't let Kara see them," I warn. I stole them from her jewelry box in her room when I went to go see Marv earlier.

She doesn't snap her hand back after I put the rings on so I hold it, enjoying the warmth and softness of her skin.

"These are Kara's?" she asks, still staring at them with wide eyes. They look so shiny in the bright sun.

"Just a placeholder," I say, hooking her arm and guiding her along the pool to where the rest of the group is sitting down at the patio table. "Until I can buy you them for real."

I don't know why I say it, but it just kind of comes out. It's not like I'd want to marry this girl. I couldn't imagine moving in with her. I'd be booking a moving truck to get the hell out of there before the cable and internet were even set up.

"They're beautiful," she says, ignoring my

comment. She's too busy admiring the insanely expensive rocks on her finger.

*They suit you perfectly.*

All kinds of servers surround us as we sit at the table. In the blink of an eye, the table is set with placemats, tropical flowers, candles, and freshly cut fruit, and a bartender is wheeling a clinking cart of alcohol over.

He pours us each a drink, starting with the ladies. Riley orders a Sex on the Beach, and she kicks me under the table when I tell her I can provide her with that.

"These yachts are pure luxury," Marv says, laying it on thick. He looks as desperate to get the sale as a teenage virgin begging his girlfriend to touch his dick. "The floors are Macassar Ebony, the finest hardwood flooring on the planet, and the bathrooms are all fitted with Balinese marble from the—"

"So," Prince Kalib says, ignoring Marv's sales pitch. He turns to Riley as he sips his eighty-year-old whiskey. "Do you like to eat marlin?"

"Yes," she says, taking a sip of her drink as she looks around, probably wondering why he's asking.

"Perfect," Prince Kalib says, lighting up in a smile. "We'll go catch some tomorrow and have them for dinner."

Riley shifts in her seat. "I thought we were just staying for lunch."

"Nonsense," Prince Kalib answers, waving a servant over. "You'll all stay the weekend."

I take a sip of my drink to hide my smile. Riley is trying to hold it together, but I can tell she's freaking out. She wants to get her money and run off to flight school, never to see any of us again.

"But it's only Friday," she says, turning white despite her suntanned skin.

"Exactly," the prince answers, trawling his soon-to-be lifeless eyes all over her. I crush an ice cube between my teeth, not liking the way this guy is looking at my 'wife.'

"We can all get to know each other," the prince says, smiling. "You can leave sometime next week."

"But we don't have any clothes or anything," Riley says, starting to sweat.

Prince Kalib waves a hand at the monstrous villa. "I have sixty women of all sizes inside. Clothes for men and women of all styles. You are welcome to take whatever you like from the communal closets."

Riley scratches her cheek, looking uncomfortable.

"We have fun first," Prince Kalib says, "and then we talk business. I want to buy yachts, but I like to know the people that I'm buying from."

"They're beautiful yachts," Riley says, leaning forward. With her wide eyes and constant swallowing, she looks like she's about to tip over into panic mode. Having to spend a few days pretending to be my husband is enough to have that effect on her. I wonder if she thinks she's getting ripped off for only getting paid a hundred and fifty thousand dollars a day to have to pretend to be my husband.

"My, *husband* and I," she says, gulping before she says the word husband, "bought one and we adore it."

"Oh, really?" Prince Kalib says, turning to me. "Do you have a harem as well, Dex?"

"No harem for me," I say, grabbing the armrest on Riley's chair and yanking her over. She lets out a little scream as she raises her drink to keep it from spilling on her. "Just this one here. She keeps me busier than two dozen girls could," I say, wrapping my arms around her. "Right, honey?"

Her body tightens under my touch, and I lean in and give her a kiss on her horrified cheek. "That's right," she answers through clenched teeth.

"She's a firecracker in the bedroom," I go on. Prince Kalib is listening with interest. "She has every position in the Kama Sutra memorized. I can't wait to get my little firecracker back to our room!"

"I'm going to be a nuclear fucking bomb when we get back to our room," she whispers, giving me a warning look.

"I love you too," I say, pretending like that's what she said.

"Love is so beautiful," Prince Kalib says, clasping his hands together as he watches us. "How did you two meet?"

We went over this at breakfast, but I can't remember if we decided on the dog park or high school sweethearts.

Riley straightens up in her chair, tucking a strand of her long brown hair behind her ear. "We were high school sweethearts," she says, nodding at him.

"I was one of the cool kids," I say, improvising, "and Riley was a total nerd."

"Really?" Prince Kalib asks. He looks surprised.

"I would have guessed that," Kara says in a harsh tone.

"She chased me for years," I say, smiling as I look at her tense face. "She chased me so much that I felt like the Road Runner. That's when I started calling her Riley Coyote. Isn't that right, honey?"

She slides her hand over mine for the show but then digs her fingernails into my palm. That part is just for me.

"It's been true love ever since," she says, giving me puppy dog eyes, but her puppy dog eyes have vicious pit bulls behind them. "Our yacht purchase has really helped take our love to the next level," she says, trying to get back to business so she can wrap this deal up and end the weekend early.

"I've heard that before," Marv says, smiling like he only does when he's in front of a client. "You're in the market for sixty yachts for your harem? What a romantic gesture."

Prince Kalib's face turns sour. "My brother, Akmal just bought each woman in his harem a Ferrari. I have to top him to save my honor."

"Sounds like a good way to spend taxpayer money," Riley mutters under her breath.

"Sixty yachts will definitely save your honor," Marv says, nodding up and down like a bobblehead on the dash of a NASCAR race car. "It will make you look like the richest and most romantic man in the world."

"How come you haven't bought me a yacht?" Kara whines to her husband. He just ignores her.

Lunch is served, and my stomach growls as I look at all of the amazing food covering the table. Riley is holding her stomach looking too sick to eat.

She's not happy with the whole situation, which makes me giddy.

I'm loving every squirm of her hot body, clench of her jaw, fidget of her hands, and flash of fire in her eyes. She has to pretend like she loves me, which for some reason is incredibly hard for her.

As soon as this is all over and Prince Kalib signs on the dotted line, she'll be gone, and Kara will give herself to me.

I should be excited for that, but I don't mind playing husband and wife for a little longer. Especially since I have Riley to warm my bed.

# CHAPTER NINE

## *RILEY*

"Four days," I groan, closing my eyes as the hot water of the shower washes over my face. *Four days pretending I like this jackass. I should have asked for a million dollars.*

I squeeze some body wash onto the loofah and rub it over my body as I go over the afternoon in my mind. It's not long before I'm gritting my teeth. *He's so frustrating!*

Dex took every opportunity he could to grab and grope me, wrapping his hard, muscular arms around my waist, grabbing my ass with his strong hands, and kissing my cheeks and neck with his soft tender lips.

My hand slides down my soapy stomach, and I let out a low moan as my fingertip finds my sweet spot. Is it so bad that I'm attracted to an arrogant pervert?

*Yes, Riley. It is.*

He's all wrong for me, but it feels so right. I must be broken. It must be his pilot's uniform. I must be drunk.

My hand slides further between my legs as I picture Dex without a shirt on, lounging by the pool. His hard abs, glistening with water as he sips on his drink and gives me that look that makes my heart race for all the wrong reasons.

*Fuck.*

I slip a finger inside my wetness and massage my breasts as I remember what it felt like when he touched them. His strong hands were firm yet gentle, making my breath catch in my throat. I pretended like I hated it, but my pussy was on fire the entire time.

It's frustrating, having dirty thoughts of your arch nemesis. I want to hate him, and I do, but I can't stop having these dirty fantasies about us having hot, wild sex.

"Mmmm," I moan, rubbing my clit as I picture Dex in the other room. Of course, we have to share a room and a bed again. Four days. I have to stay strong for four days.

But I only have to stay strong when I'm with him. Alone in the shower on the other hand...

"Oh, God," I moan as I slide another finger in deep. I press my forehead against the cold shower tiles as I imagine him walking in when he does.

"What the fuck?!" I scream as he opens the door and casually walks in. I quickly make a hand bikini as he strolls to the toilet, thankfully keeping his eyes off of the steamy glass wall of the shower. It's the only thing standing between him and my naked body.

"What are you doing in here?" I yell as he lifts

up the lid of the toilet and unbuckles his shorts.

"What does it look like I'm doing?" he asks with a chuckle.

I slide the door open a sliver and reach out, grabbing the folded towel off of the shelf. "It looks like you're pulling your dick out," I say as I yank the towel in and wrap it around me. "Get the fuck out of here!"

"I have to pee," he says casually, shrugging as he looks down.

He glances over his shoulder as he starts peeing. "Your towel is getting wet."

The jets of the shower have already soaked it. "Actually, it's *your* towel. *I'm* keeping the dry one."

"We can share the last towel," he says. I can hear the grin in his voice. "I don't mind that at all."

"Well, I do!" I shout. I'm in complete disbelief over the brazenness of his actions. To think I was actually fantasizing about this jerk.

"Leave your panties," he says, glancing down at my pile of clothes in the corner. My lacy yellow underwear is on the floor, visible for him to see. "I'll dry off with those, if they're not already soaking wet from seeing me shirtless all afternoon."

"Why don't you dry off with all of that hot air coming out of your mouth?" I ask, sticking my head out of the door. It's not the best comeback, but he's kind of caught me off guard.

"Did you just call me hot?" he asks, smiling as he glances over his shoulder.

I can only stare at him in disbelief. "I can't tell if you're delusional or stupid."

"Let me know when you figure it out," he says. He turns and points to his dick that's hidden by his body. "Want to shake it for me?"

He flushes the toilet when I just glare at him, not answering his question. He then washes his hands, watching me through the reflection in the mirror.

"Need some help washing your breasts?" he asks, strutting to the door. He stops in front of the shower with a smirk on his lips. "I'm an expert."

"No!" I shout at the top of my lungs. "I need some help getting a pervert out of my bathroom while I'm taking a shower!"

"I'll take that as a 'next time,'" he says, laughing.

I throw the shampoo bottle at him and hit him in the shoulder.

He laughs as he points at my leg. "You missed a spot."

He hurries out as I grab the conditioner. I launch it at him, but it hits the back of the door as he quickly closes it.

I'm not sure if I'm angrier at him for trying to see me naked or at myself for getting turned on by it.

I turn off the hot water faucet and hold my breath as the shower turns freezing cold.

*Only cold showers from now on.*

"Wow," Dex says when I walk into the room before dinner. His jaw is hanging down, looking like it's unhinged from his skull.

I hide my grin, pretending that I don't care

what he thinks. I found a beautiful summer dress in the communal closet, which is pretty much a warehouse stocked with the nicest designer clothes on the planet. The dress is bright red, and I grabbed some sexy Louboutins to match.

It's almost dinnertime, and we have to go over our notes. I dig them out of my purse and unfold the papers. "Where did you go to school?" I ask.

He just ignores me as his eyes wander all over my body, darting from my breasts, to my legs, to my breasts, to my waist, and then back to my breasts.

I don't think I'm the prettiest girl in the world, but I did make sure I looked hot as fuck before leaving the bathroom. Dex and I are fighting a war, and I believe in torturing my enemies.

I'm thrilled that it seems to be working, but we still have work to do. My future is on the line.

"Where did you go to school?" I repeat. I roll my eyes and turn the page when he doesn't answer. *Is that drool on the side of his mouth?*

"What is my favorite color?" I ask.

"My favorite color is red," he says, staring at me.

"That's not what it says in the notes," I say, shaking the papers.

"I don't care," he says, swallowing hard. "It's my favorite color now."

"Ugh," I say, tossing the notes on the bed. "Let's just go."

Dex stands up and now it's my turn to gawk and gasp. He's wearing fitted gray slacks with a tight black button up shirt that clings to his broad shoulders and round biceps. A gray tie hangs loose around his thick neck, and for a split second, I picture grabbing it in my fist and pulling his lips down onto mine.

His blue eyes are looking brighter than ever against his tanned skin, and his hair is in a style I haven't seen it in before-gelled and combed to the side. I like it.

A lot.

He slides his hand on my lower back as we leave, and although I specifically said there will be no touching, I let it go. He is supposed to be my husband, and husbands touch their wives. It's definitely *not* because I like it.

We bicker on the way down to the dining room, basically me getting pissed that he still hasn't memorized our notes from breakfast. All of that is pushed to the side when we walk into the room and greet Prince Kalib, Marv, and Kara with smiles on our faces.

After a quick drink, we sit down at the gorgeous oak table under the minivan-sized chandelier that's dangling over our heads. The room is pure luxury, from the large Japanese vases in the corners that look so old that I wouldn't be surprised if they were once owned by a Samurai, to the solid gold silverware that I consider sneaking into my purse.

Marv tries to bring up the yachts again as the servers bring out salads and wine. Prince Kalib isn't having any of it. He turns away from my boss and locks his eyes on me.

"Where did you grow up, Riley?" he asks, never taking his eyes off of me as he tastes the wine and then nods to the waiter who's holding the bottle.

Dex and I had agreed this morning on the story that I was born in New Hampshire and he was born in LA. We met on vacation in Miami and decided to stay for good after falling in love.

Dex answers before I can open my mouth. *Shit.*

"We grew up together in Wisconsin," he says, nodding at the prince. "Isn't that right, honey?"

I squeeze my napkin under the table as my chest aches. I have a sudden sour taste in my mouth as the entire table turns to look at me. He's done exactly what I was worried he was going to do. He's gone off script. He's gone rogue!

I have six-hundred thousand dollars on the line and he's freeballing it! Well, he's going to pay for every word.

"That's true," I say, gulping as I nod. "That's where Dex joined the Air Force. I was so worried about him when he was enrolled."

Dex is watching me carefully, probably wondering what my game is. He's about to find out.

"I was so happy when he got discharged," I say, taking his hand in mine. "That's a great story, honey. Why don't you tell them?"

*Checkmate.*

Dex furrows his brow as he pulls his hand away from mine. He wipes the corner of his mouth with his napkin as his face turns serious.

"I didn't realize you were in the Air Force, Dex," Prince Kalib says. "Why did they make you leave?"

I've been wondering why he got discharged from the Air Force ever since we first met. I lean in, excited to find out why.

"My little Riley Coyote was so worried about me that she traded her body for my safety," he says.

"What?" Marv grunts, tilting his head as he looks at Dex.

"Yeah, what?" I repeat, staring at him.

Dex nods, looking like he's getting choked up. "Riley slept with my commanding officer in exchange for my discharge. Some wives will say they'll do anything for their husband, but not many wives will get naked and spread their legs on a pool table in the back of a seedy bar to keep their husband safe. My Riley Coyote took an old saggy man cock for me, and I won't forget it. Ever."

I'm not even mad. I just watch him with admiration as he takes my hand and gives it a gentle squeeze. Here I thought I had him in checkmate and he steals my queen. He's a master at this game.

"That's so romantic," Prince Kalib says, wiping the corner of his eye.

We finish our salads, and all hell breaks loose when Prince Kalib excuses himself to go to the bathroom.

"What the hell are you two playing at?" Marv screeches, trying to keep his voice down but failing miserably.

"She's wearing my rings!" Kara hisses, pointing at my finger. I keep my hands on the table. My left hand is closing except for my middle finger.

"I'm just borrowing them," I say defensively.

Kara tugs on Marv's sleeve. "She's wearing my rings!" she whines like a spoiled little brat.

Marv sighs. "I'll buy you new ones when we get home. Like you don't have enough," he mutters under his breath.

Kara shoots me an ugly look. "Just throw them in the garbage when you're done with them. They're tainted now."

"I want everyone to act normal," Marv says, squeezing his hand into a fist. "You guys are blowing this!"

"He loves us!" Dex says, shrugging his broad shoulders. "Don't worry, we both want to sell the yachts and get our rewards too."

"What's your reward?" I ask, looking at him sideways.

"Yeah," Kara asks, smirking at us. "Why don't you tell her, Dex?"

His body turns rigid as he glares back at her.

"Dex?" I whisper. "What's your reward?"

"Will you guys stop?" Dex asks, looking around in a panic. "He's going to hear you!"

"Dex?" I say once again. He's pretending he doesn't hear me.

"Who's ready for the main course?" Prince Kalib asks, rubbing his hands together as he walks back into the dining room.

We all swallow our scowls and flash him fake smiles. "I am!" I say, smiling like a crazy person.

The waiters serve us grilled fish and veggies on silver platters. *Real* silver platters.

Prince Kalib asks me a million questions as I cut my fish, trying to take out the tiny slivers of bone. He seems to be quite taken with me.

And by the way Dex is clenching his teeth, muttering under his breath and sneering at Prince Kalib, it seems he's quite taken with me too. I'd laugh in his face if I wasn't putting on a show for the prince.

By dessert, Dex has had enough.

"You took gymnastics as a child," Prince Kalib says as he sinks his fork into the crème brûlée. "Are you still flexible?"

"All right," Dex says, springing up from the table so fast his chair skids back across the floor. "I think it's time to go to bed."

"So early?" Prince Kalib asks, looking at his diamond-encrusted watch.

"Yes," Dex growls back, locking eyes on him.

"We're sorry to cut the evening short," I say, tossing my napkin on the table. "Dex has a nightly tradition where he calls his mother every night before bed so she can sing him a lullaby. At first I thought it was very strange and creepy that a grown man needs to be sung a lullaby by his mommy, but now I think it's sweet. A little bit strange but sweet."

Dex doesn't look like he's in the mood for any more games.

"Let's go," he mouths to me.

His face is red and he looks unpredictable at the moment. I'm afraid he's going to blow the whole charade, so I say goodnight to everyone and go with him.

"Geez," I say, yanking my hand out of his when we're in the hallway. "What is your problem?"

He's steaming mad as he paces around while I rub my wrists. "The fucking nerve of that guy!" he hisses before kicking a plant. "He's been hitting on you all night!"

"Are you jealous?" I ask, grinning in triumph at him.

"No!" he says, snorting out a laugh. "As if. He thinks you're with me. It's rude."

"And you're jealous," I say, biting my bottom lip as I watch him kick the base of the plant again.

"It's not the plant's fault," I say, giggling at him.

"There you are," Prince Kalib says as he turns the corner.

"What do you want?" Dex asks, puffing out his chest.

I grab his flexed arm and pull him behind me. He wouldn't have budged if he didn't let me move him. "Please excuse my husband. He has the temperament of a toddler when he stays up past his bedtime. What can we do for you, Prince Kalib?"

"You have done so much already, Mrs. Riley," he says, smiling warmly at me. He turns to Dex and stands up straight. "I was wondering if I could have a moment of your husband's time."

I raise an eyebrow as I turn to look at Dex. His shoulders drop, the aggression gone as confusion takes its place. "Uh, sure," he says, rubbing his chin.

"This way please," Prince Kalib says, motioning down the hall with his hands.

Dex turns to me and shrugs. "I'll meet you back at the room."

"Sure, whatever," I say, trying to seem like I don't give a fuck. But I'm lying. I give lots of fucks. I'm secretly upset that he's leaving me by myself.

As frustrating as his company is, it's also kind of fun.

It still doesn't stop me from flipping him the bird as he walks away.

Dex is still my enemy after all.

# CHAPTER TEN

## *DEX*

I walk down the extravagant hallway keeping my eye on the prince even though we're passing paintings that should probably be hanging inside the Louvre. I don't like this guy.

I don't like the way he keeps dragging his rich eyes over Riley's body like she's a piece of meat.

If anyone is eating that steak, it's gonna be me.

"Your wife is very beautiful," Prince Sleeze says, smiling at me over his shoulder. "You are a very lucky man."

"I know," I say, my voice tight. I don't know where he's taking me, but it's taking forever. This place is like a maze with its long hallways and millions of doors. I wonder what the people of his country would say about this extravagance that they financed. I'm sure they would be thrilled to hear all about it while they ration their dinners.

"I'm a very generous man," Prince Kalib says, placing a palm on his chest. "I would like to share what I have with you."

"I'll take that helicopter that's parked on the roof," I say without hesitation. I've had my eye on it ever since I was flying and saw it on the horizon.

He laughs. "I was thinking of something a little softer and wetter," he says, raising an eyebrow.

*If he tries to kiss me, I'm knocking him out.*

I take a step back and plant my feet wide, just in case.

"Why don't I show you what I mean?" he says, smiling wide. He turns around the corner and walks down the long hall. I can hear a muted beat playing from somewhere.

Prince Kalib stops at two huge double doors that are intricately carved with naked women. Even the two brass handles are in the shape of breasts.

I'm about to ask him where I can buy doors like that when he grabs the boob-shaped handles.

"I'd like to share with you, Dex," he says, grinning as he turns the handles. "This is what I have to offer."

He swings the doors open, and the loud house music pours out into the hallway. I swallow hard as I step to the side and look inside.

*The harem.*

The inside looks like a private club complete with bars, leather sofas, a dance floor, and numerous stripper poles, but that's nothing compared to *who's* inside-sixty of the most beautiful women in the world all dressed in lingerie, dancing, grinding, kissing, groping. I'm instantly hard as my eyes dart around the room trying to take in the abundance of flesh and curves on display.

I swallow hard when I see two hot blondes making out on the couch, and let out a whimper as I see a gorgeous Asian girl taking a shot from between the naked tits of a beautiful Russian girl.

"Come in," a sexy black girl calls to me, waving me in from the bar. All sixty girls turn to me and smile, waving me in to join their party.

I'm about to step in for a drink (I don't want to be rude by turning down their invitation) when Prince Kalib closes the doors.

He's grinning as he leans against it and watches me. "Do you want me to share with you?"

I try to say 'yes please,' but it comes out as a whimper.

"I'm happy to," he says, smiling widely. "As long as you share with me."

My heartbeat turns sluggish as I turn to him with a rolling stomach. I don't like where this is going.

I pull out a pack of gum from my shorts. "I can share my gum with you."

"That's very generous," he says, laughing tightly. "But I'm afraid I'm not interested in your gum. Your wife, however…"

He lets the thought hover between us, polluting the air in the hallway.

I loosen my collar as heat flushes through my body.

*I wonder if I can break through that door by only using his head?*

"You don't have to answer now," he says, showing me his palms. "It's just an idea. The women are always ready to go, whenever you are."

He smiles as he puts a hand on my shoulder and walks me back in the direction we came.

"Sixty tight pussies, one hundred and twenty beautiful breasts, six hundred skilled fingers," he says, nodding. "Sixty women in exchange for one. That's a very generous offer."

I gulp as I walk down the hall, staring at the ugly carpet.

Would I trade Riley for sixty women? Yesterday, I would have traded her for a pack of Tic Tacs, but now I'm not so sure. I'm getting protective of my fake wife.

No matter how much she seems to hate me.

Still, sixty women on their knees. It's a once in a lifetime opportunity.

But so is meeting a girl like Riley.

My head is still swirling with a thousand thoughts as I quietly open the door. I laugh under my breath when I see Riley lying in the bed. It's not the beautiful sight of her brown hair on the pillow next to mine that makes me chuckle, it's the barricade she's erected between her side of the bed and mine. The empty drawers of the dresser are stacked in a line down the middle of the bed.

"What did the prince want?" she asks without turning her head around to look at me.

"He wanted to show me his cigar collection," I lie. I could get her all worked up by telling her what I really saw, but we're stuck in the same room for the night, and I don't want her to get all riled up again. Who wants to sleep in the same room as an angry lioness?

She finally turns. Her makeup is off and she looks just as incredible without it. She's a natural beauty, and the makeup only seems to take away from her angelic face.

"You don't stink," she says, sniffing the air.

"That's the first compliment you've ever given me," I say, smiling as I pull off my tie.

She laughs. "That's hardly a compliment."

I toss my tie on the back of the chair and grin. "I'll take what I can get."

She turns back around as I start to unbutton my shirt, but her body is rising and falling as her breathing speeds up.

I strip to my boxer briefs that I borrowed from the huge communal closet and slide in between the sheets. The dresser drawers rattle as my body makes the mattress bounce.

"What's with the border?" I ask, staring up at the dark ceiling. "Are you afraid that you can't trust yourself around me?"

She lets out a mocking laugh. "Please. It's to stop your wandering hands."

I smile. "How was your day?"

I can hear her thinking. "Why are you asking?" she asks after a brief silence.

"Husbands usually ask their wives how their day was at the end of it."

"And pretend husbands and wives?" she asks.

"They usually have sex."

She laughs.

"Hot, dirty, rough sex," I say, feeling my dick

start to harden.

"You're such an idiot," she says. There's a lightness in her voice. She seems to be getting used to my crude words. I'm wearing her down. Just a few more years of this, and maybe she'll take the wall on the bed down.

"I may be an idiot," I say, grinning. "But you're the one on the wrong side of the bed."

"No, I'm not."

"Well, one of us is."

"Goodnight, Dex," she says after a giggle. "Better bring your A-game tomorrow."

"Goodnight, Riley Coyote," I say, staring at the drawers between us, wishing that I could see her beautiful face one more time before I close my eyes. "And remember, if you dream of me, I'd like it if you keep those sexy red shoes on."

"I don't normally get nightmares, but thanks."

I drift off to sleep with a smile on my lips.

# CHAPTER ELEVEN

## *RILEY*

"Yes," I moan as Dex slides his big palms down my legs, giving me goosebumps. His hands stop at the bright red shoes still on my feet and he smirks. I'm wearing the shoes-and only the shoes.

"Fuck, you're sexy," he groans as he kisses a trail down from my ankles to the red Louboutins on my feet. "I'm going to fuck you extra hard for keeping these on."

I gulp as my eyes wander down his muscular body, taking in every inch of hard muscle, every deep ridge and sexy line of his chest and abs. My eyes continue past his shredded abs to the perfect V that's carved into his pelvis. I moan as my eyes stop at his trimmed pubic hair before continuing down to the main attraction.

His cock is huge-thick and long as it points up at the ceiling waiting to please me.

My pussy clenches as he separates my legs and

climbs over me, making my heart thump. I reach down and wrap my fingers around his cock, moaning as I realize how big he actually is.

"Stick it in me," I beg. I can hear the desperation in my voice.

My wet lips part as he drags his tip up my wet folds, making my back arch. I reach for him, holding him as close as I can as he guides his delicious cock into my tight hole.

"Yes!" I scream, already feeling an orgasm coming on. "Fuck yes! Just like that!"

His beautiful face is in front of mine as he thrusts inside of me over and over again. "Just like what?" he asks.

His cock feels so good but he's slowing down. "Just like what?"

It's then that my eyes pop open and cruel reality comes crashing down. Dex is leaning over the barricade I made, grinning as he watches me. "Just like what?"

"Nothing," I shout, yanking the blankets up to my neck. Luckily, I didn't strip naked while having my sex dream.

"It didn't sound like nothing," he says, laughing as he sits up on the bed.

I glance at the clock before squeezing my eyes shut. It's the middle of the night. How loud was I that he woke up? What exactly did I say? Is it possible to actually die of embarrassment?

These questions and more are racing through my head as he reaches over and taps my shoulder. "Sounds like you were having an exciting dream," he says with a knowing voice.

"I wasn't," I lie.

"What were you dreaming about?" he asks. His voice sounds like he's smirking. I hate him.

"Nothing. Leave me alone."

"Fine," he says, climbing back under the sheets. "I'll leave you alone. You seem to be all hot and bothered anyway."

I squeeze my eyes shut as my stomach hardens. My ears feel impossibly hot like they always do when I'm mortified.

How could I have a sex dream about Dex? Even my subconscious is betraying me. First it was my body, now it's my mind. Can't every part of me see that this guy is all wrong for me? He's pure evil. Sexy as hell, but pure evil.

I finally start to loosen up a little when I think that he's dropped it and gone back to sleep. He's been quiet for a few minutes but I should have known better. This is *Dex* after all.

"Can I ask you one question about your dream?" he asks.

"No."

He asks it anyways.

"Did you leave your red shoes on for me?"

I explode out of bed like the mattress is on fire and grab my pillow.

"Where are you going?" he asks, grinning as he watches me storm across the room.

"I'm sleeping in the bathroom!" I snap.

He laughs as I toss my pillow on the tiles and grab the door handle.

"Don't forget to keep your shoes on."

I slam the door in his face.

I feel like a prisoner about to walk onto a pirate ship. I'm surrounded by enemies, but I have a big dumb fake smile plastered on my face.

The yacht is ready for us, but I'm standing on the dock as long as I can. I don't want to be trapped with these people for a second longer than I have to be.

"I hope you brought your bikini," Prince Kalib says, giving me a creepy look, and making me glad I wore my shorts and tank top over my bathing suit. "You're going to need it!"

I cringe as he steps off the dock and onto the yacht. He's taking us deep sea fishing so we can catch our dinner.

Marv walks up next, looking like he'd rather be anywhere but stepping onto Prince Kalib's boat. "It's time to earn your commission," he says, leaning in and growling in my ear. "Help me sell these yachts. I have other business to take care of this weekend."

His lovely wife Kara follows him in, glaring at me as she steps onto the boat. "I'm watching you," she whispers, pointing two fingers at her eyes and then sticking her index finger at me. Maybe I'll get lucky and she'll get eaten by a shark.

My biggest enemy is last. Dex saunters up the dock looking sinfully good in his boardshorts. A white tank top is tossed over his shoulder, and he's got those aviator glasses on that drive me nuts. I'd check him out if I wasn't still embarrassed about last night.

I wince as he approaches, wanting to cover

my face with my hands. I glance at the deep water, wondering if anyone would notice if I sunk to the bottom and never came back out.

"Good morning," he says, grinning from ear to ear. "Sweet dreams last night?"

"Shut up."

He tilts his head to the side. "Why so cranky? Did you not sleep well?"

My ears start to burn as he chuckles. "You were tossing and turning all night. Actually, it was more like moaning and writhing."

"I hate you."

He just laughs. "Here," he says, taking my hand. He opens my clenched fingers and drops a tiny pill inside my palm. "Take this or you'll be puking the whole boat ride."

"Thanks," I say, swallowing the Gravol. It's another reason why I'm still on the dock. I wanted to wait until the last moment before getting on the rocking yacht.

"Don't be embarrassed. It's just a little dream," he says, smiling for real at me. "I dream about us all of the time." He closes his eyes and takes a deep breath. "I'm doing it right now."

"Stop," I say, feeling my ears getting really hot now.

"Oh fuck," he says, tilting his head to the side. His muscles are flexed and I secretly wish I could see what he's seeing. "Wow. Your legs are spread so far apart. I didn't realize you're so flexible. You're almost doing the splits."

I slap his arm and he opens his eyes, laughing as he looks down at me.

"Knock it off," I say. I walk past him, but

then stop when I reach the yacht. I turn to him with a grin. "By the way, I *can* do the splits. You can imagine me all you want, but I'm even more flexible than *that*."

I hear a loud gulp from behind me as I step onto the boat.

The boat is jerking around in the rough open sea making me thankful for that Gravol. *When is this supposed to start being fun?*

Prince Kalib is driving the boat, Marv is yelling into his satellite phone, Kara is puking into a bucket (well, that part is fun), and Dex is sitting across from me staring at my breasts which are bouncing and jiggling around in my bikini top.

"The view is over there," I say, pointing to the ocean.

"My eyes are perfectly fine right here," he says, staring at my chest.

I roll my eyes as I grab my tank top and slip it on, blocking his view.

"Ahh," he sighs, looking disappointed. "You never let me have any fun."

"Not if it involves me getting traumatized," I say, licking the salt water off my lips.

The boat's engines die down to a low rumble and Prince Kalib pops his head out of the Captain's cabin. "I think we're going to get lucky with this spot," he says, only addressing me.

"At least someone is getting lucky," Dex

mumbles.

The prince cuts the engines and starts setting up the fishing poles, baiting the hooks and doing whatever he has to do so we can get this day over with.

Kara groans as she drops her head back. Her face looks as green as the puke sloshing inside the bucket on her lap.

"How are you feeling, Kara?" I ask her in a sing-song voice, smiling extra wide at her.

"I feel how you look," she says, spitting into the bucket as she glares at me.

"Some raw fish will settle your stomach," Dex says.

Her cheeks bulge as big as her eyes as she starts heaving. Dex gives me a wink as she starts another violent round of puking.

Marv finally gets off his phone and joins us with the prince by the fishing poles. It's a hot, beautiful day, and although I'd rather be on this boat with literally anyone else in the world than these three people, I'm still excited to go deep sea fishing.

My father vanished from my life when I was a toddler, and my mother wasn't the fishing type. I've always wanted to try it but never bothered to go on my own. So, I'm pretty excited to hold a fishing rod for the first time. Well, second time if you count the aisles of Walmart.

Dex is a natural, of course. He takes a rod, baits the hook, and casts it like a pro as I'm trying to handle mine without getting the hook stuck in my leg.

"Like this," he says, as he places his fishing rod into the holder on the boat. My breath seizes as he comes up behind me and slides his hands down my arms.

I swallow hard, staring at the water but seeing nothing as I feel his hard chest graze the top of my back. His warm breath tickles my neck as he shows me how to hold it properly.

"Like that," he whispers, placing my fingers on the handle. "Just like you're holding a—"

The look I give him over my shoulder shuts him up.

"How do I make the hook go far out like you did?" I ask. I really want to catch something, and the best I can do is let the hook fall right beside the boat where exactly zero fish are swimming.

He moves his warm body a little closer and tightens his grip on my forearms, making me light-headed. I have to focus on the instructions coming out of his mouth, but I can only seem to focus on his big biceps curled around me, his low voice growling in my ear, and his heart beating against my back.

"Got it?" he asks, stepping back after he explains how to do the motion.

"Yes," I lie. I don't got it.

And that's clear when I try to cast the hook like he did. The rod sails out of my hands and plops into the water.

"That's a start," he says as we both start laughing. I look at the prince to see if he saw, but he's setting up the rods with Marv on the other side of the boat.

"Try again," Dex says, handing me another one.

He gives me a few pointers, mainly to keep my hands closed, and I try again. This time the hook sails through the air and lands a few feet from his.

"Yay!" I squeal, jumping up in the air.

"Great job!" he says, smiling as he holds up his hand for a high-five. I slap my palm against his, and he closes his hand around mine, holding it for an extra moment.

Something electric passes between us, and I yank my hand back before I get burned. "Thanks," I mumble, turning toward the ocean as I hold the rod with both hands.

I lean against the edge of the boat, watching the sparkling ocean as we wait for an unlucky fish to bite. Dex stands beside me in a comfortable silence, enjoying the view as well, and I realize that this is the first time we've been together for more than five minutes without getting at each other's throats. It's kinda nice.

"Have you ever been fishing before?" I ask after a while.

"Yeah," he says, running a hand through his hair as he takes a deep breath. "I lived in Alaska when I was a kid, and my dad would take me fishing during the summer."

I jerk my head back in surprise. "Alaska?" I spit out, staring at him in shock. "I didn't know that."

He smiles a sad smile. "I haven't been there since I was seven-years-old."

"Is your dad from Alaska?" I ask, wanting to know everything about him. Not because I care, but to use for future ammunition in our war. Definitely *not* because I care.

"*Was* from Alaska," he says, gazing out at the ocean with an empty stare. "He died two days before my seventh birthday."

"I'm sorry," I say, dropping my head. The

look on his face is so raw and full of emotion that I suddenly feel like I'm an intruder who stepped into the wrong room and is witnessing something deeply personal.

"It's okay," he says, his voice thicker than usual. "My father was Alaskan born and raised. A real mountain of a man. You wouldn't find a tougher guy, but when he was around my mother he was pure jelly. He was so in love with her."

"Was she from Alaska too?"

"No," he says, shaking his head. "She was from Richmond, Virginia. She moved up to Alaska to live with him but when he died she moved us back down to her home so she could be close to her family. I haven't been back up to Alaska since."

"What happened to him?" I ask softly. "It's okay if you don't want to tell me."

He looks down at his hand, which is picking at the rubber ridges of the fishing pole. "Cancer," he says, the dreaded word catching in his throat. "I hero-worshiped him when I was a kid, and I was forced to watch the man who lifted me on his wide shoulders like I weighed nothing waste away to a skeleton. Three months after the diagnosis, he was dead."

My chest aches as I listen to his heartbreaking words. He takes a deep breath as he stares out at the ocean, trying to steel his emotions.

I'm not as good at that as he is. My eyes start to water as soreness sits in my throat. "I'm sorry," I say, inching a little closer to him. Our arms touch, and for the first time, I keep it there. "I know how much it sucks to grow up without a dad."

"Really?" he asks, looking down at me with soft eyes.

I nod as my shoulders droop down. "He ran out on my mom when I was a toddler."

"Prick," he mutters under his breath. "I find it hard to believe that someone would leave you."

His words take me by surprise, and I'm about to ask him what he means when my fishing rod jerks forward. I tighten my grip around the handle as I look down at the tight fishing line.

"I caught something!" I shout out in surprise.

Dex secures his fishing pole and rushes behind me, supporting me with his strong arms. "Okay," he says, as my breath races. My heart is beating so fast.

"Lower your rod fast," he says, helping me. "Now quickly turn the reel."

The beast on the other end is so strong. My flexed arms are burning as I try to reel him in.

"You do it," I say, worried that I'll screw it up.

"No way," he says, shaking his head. "You got this, Riley Coyote. Just keep doing what I showed you."

It takes forever, and I'm exhausted with my arms on fire, but I finally get the beast to the surface.

"Holy crap!" Marv shouts as he looks overboard. "That's got to be at least thirteen feet!"

"What is it?" I ask, gritting my teeth as I struggle to turn the reel.

"A marlin," Prince Kalib says as he looks overboard.

"It feels like Godzilla," I say between ragged breaths.

I take a peek overboard and gasp when I see the large marlin thrashing around in the water, swinging his long nose-sword around like a pirate.

"Dex," I gasp, looking up at him as sweat drips down my temple. "He's too big for me."

"I'm right here," he says, wrapping his arms around me for support. "Let's do this together."

The load becomes lighter as Dex shoulders the bulk of it. With the strain off of me and on Dex, I can enjoy the moment more. My senses are heightened as adrenaline rushes through me. I can feel the ridges of the handle against my palms, I can taste the salt from the water on my dry lips, I can smell Dex's musky scent around me, I can hear the waves slamming against the side of the boat, and finally, I can see the shiny blue marlin as it's pulled on-board.

I fall backward, completely exhausted, but luckily Dex is there to catch me. He holds me up as he smiles in my ear. "Great job!" he whispers.

My happiness is short lived as I look down at the spectacular creature thrashing around on the floor of the boat. He's huge-much taller than Dex-with beautiful blue stripes on his silver belly. He swings his long sword-shaped nose as he flails around in confusion. He looked so majestic when I caught a glimpse of him in the water, but now he just looks sad and desperate as he slowly dies at my feet.

"He's a beauty," Marv says, slapping his thigh as Prince Kalib takes the hook out of the marlin's lip. "I've never seen one so big!"

"I'll get my knife," Prince Kalib says, sounding giddy as he rushes to the other side of the boat.

"I'll get my camera," Marv says, running after him.

My body turns rigid as guilt and horror sets in. My stomach is rolling with nerves as I watch him with my vision blurred. He was the king of the ocean, and now he's going to be stuffed and mounted on the wall over Marv's couch.

"Are you okay?" Dex whispers as he studies my face.

I'm too upset to talk, so I just shake my head as my lips close into a tight line. My chin trembles as the stunning animal's movements slow and his mouth opens and closes, his eyes glossing over into a dull haze.

Dex steps in front of me and lowers his face so that our eyes are level. "Want me to throw him back in?" he whispers.

I just nod. It's all I can do.

In a heartbeat, he turns around and slides his powerful arms under the marlin's silver belly. With a savage grunt, he lifts the creature up and gently tosses it overboard.

Tears of relief well up behind my eyelids as I watch it swim away unharmed. I lean on the boat, holding onto the edge with trembling hands as it disappears below the surface.

"Thank you," I whisper to Dex as he stands beside me, watching the water.

My heart picks up again as he gives me a slow smile and a little wink.

"Where did it go?" Marv asks in a panic.

Dex turns to him, sheltering me with his body. "He was bucking so hard that he jumped overboard."

I smile as I hide behind him, admiring his strong back.

This doesn't change anything. He's still a jerk. He's still my enemy.

I still hate him.

And I'll be sure to tell him that as soon as I can stop smiling.

# CHAPTER TWELVE

## *RILEY*

*This will get his heart pumping.* I look in the mirror and shake my head. This morning I wanted Dex's heart to stop for good, and now I want to get it pumping.

"What is wrong with you?" I ask the reflection in the mirror. "He is the enemy."

I pick up the sweet-smelling perfume on the counter, ignoring the disapproving face in the mirror as I spray it on my neck. *I wonder if the enemy would like this smell.*

"What?" I ask the reflection staring back at me. "It's chemical warfare. Definitely *not* trying to impress him."

I step onto my toes and take one last look at my outfit before walking to the door of the bathroom. I picked a fitted yellow dress from the communal closet that I'm sure Dex will love.

Not that I care. I hate it when he's constantly

staring at me.

He sits up on the bed with wide eyes when I walk into the room, and I have to turn to hide my smile.

"Wow," he says, gawking at me. "Riley Coyote, you look absolutely phenomenal."

"Thank you," I say, feeling sexy in the tight dress.

He grins as he glances at the wall of drawers down the middle of the bed. "Maybe we can put the drawers back in the dresser where they belong," he says, biting his bottom lip as he looks me up and down.

"Only if you promise to keep *your* drawers where they belong."

"On the floor?" he asks, smirking.

"Try again."

"Stuffed in your mouth while I take you from behi—"

"Okay!" I say, raising my hand as I interrupt him. "You were a gentleman for half a second before you blew it. Congratulations. It's a new record."

He laughs as he gets off the bed and follows me to the door.

"I'll be a gentleman all night if I get to see you slip out of that dress after," he says as we leave the room.

"I'm sure you will," I say, flipping my hair back as I look up at him. "But you'll be back to your asshole ways in the morning."

"Probably," he says as he laughs. "But things will be different because you'll be in love with me."

"Oh, really?"

"Really," he says, looking sexy as hell as he

nods his head. "You're already in love with me. That's why you hate me so much. You're suppressing your feelings of attraction, and they're coming out as hate."

I want to wipe the arrogant cocky grin off his face. With my lips.

He may have a sliver of a point there. I'm not in love with him. At all. I'm not even sure I like him. But I do hate him less than I did yesterday.

He's growing on me. Like a big brutish wart, he's growing on me.

Marv intercepts us in the hallway before we can walk into the dining room for dinner. His face is red, and it's not from the sun-filled day. He looks pissed.

"This has gone on long enough," he says, trying to shout and keep his voice low at the same time. Somehow, he does it. "You two have to help me out and sell him those fucking yachts. That's why you're here!"

I jerk my body to the side, dodging the index finger that he's waving around.

"It's time for you to earn your commission," he says to me with a fierce glare. He turns to Dex and narrows his eyes on him. "And it's time for you to earn what we agreed upon."

I still haven't found out what that is, and by the way Dex looks all closed up and rigid, it appears that I'm not going to be finding out now.

"Good evening," Prince Kalib says from inside the dining room when he sees us. "Come in, come in."

"I mean it," Marv says, rubbing his forehead like he's trying to massage his brain through his thick skull. "Let's close this deal so we can get the fuck out of here."

When Marv turns, he's a completely different man. "Is that steak I smell?" he asks, opening his arms with a big smile on his face. "My stomach is rumbling. That smells delicious!"

Prince Kalib looks pleased as he walks over. "Go get yourself a drink," he says, waving Marv to the bar. "I want to drink in my lovely guests."

Marv shoots us a warning look before charging over to the bar and sulking on a stool.

"You look ravishing," Prince Kalib says, slowly looking me up and down. He grabs my shoulders and kisses me on both cheeks. I can see Dex's body stiffen out of the corner of my eye. *Did he just growl?*

"You two are so in love," Prince Kalib says, giving us each a warm smile as he looks at us. His eyes settle back on me, and I can hear Dex's violent breathing from here. "It's so wonderful to see true love."

I nod, swallowing hard. It's time to put my business hat on. It's time to sell this spoiled Prince way too many yachts.

"You know," I say, hooking my arm around Dex's, "our relationship really bloomed when we bought our Gladstone yacht. Everything from the king-sized bed in the master bedroom, the granite countertops in the bathrooms, to the five gas fireplaces on-board really helped sail our love into a new direction." I glance up at Dex to see if he's impressed by my sales pitch. I mentioned three features *and* slipped in a pun!

"Laying it on a little thick," he whispers.

He doesn't know what he's talking about.

"Do you have anyone special in your life, Prince Kalib?" I ask him. "Someone who you could watch the sunset with aboard a Gladstone yacht, the second largest luxury yacht producers in the world?"

"Yeah, he's got sixty of them," Dex mutters beside me.

I flash him a dirty look and then turn back to the prince with a smile brewing on my lips. "Anyone?"

"Not yet," he says, smiling sadly at me. "But I have my eye on a special someone."

Dex tenses up beside me. "I'm sure you do."

I watch in confusion as the two men stare each other down like two alpha males about to fight over a steak.

*Wait a minute. Am I a steak?*

"Let's eat," Prince Kalib says, breaking first. He waves us into the room and Dex reluctantly walks in.

"What is going on?" I whisper to him when the prince is out of earshot.

Dex just ignores me and marches off to the bar.

"That was rude," I whisper to myself.

Kara is sitting at the table, only looking slightly better than she did on the boat. Her hair is a blonde mess, her eyes are bloodshot, and her skin still has a slight shade of green that I'm hoping is now permanent.

She gives me her patented evil glare as I walk by.

This time I stop and face her. "What's the matter, Kara? Not used to puking *before* the meal?"

She opens her mouth to respond but then

gags instead. I giggle as she jumps out of the chair and runs out of the room clutching her stomach as she dry heaves.

"Is she okay?" Prince Kalib asks, pointing at the doorway.

"She's fine," Marv says, not bothering to look up.

"I was hoping to serve you some barbecued marlin," Prince Kalib says, shaking his head in disappointment, "but unfortunately you know what happened there. Our dinner escaped."

*Thank God.* He's probably in the middle of the ocean right now, sword fighting a shark with his nose to save his princess. And it's all because of Dex.

Kara still hasn't returned when we sit down for dinner, and Marv doesn't bother to go check on her. I can't blame him there. He's probably used to her spitting vile out of her mouth every time she speaks, so he looks unfazed.

Prince Kalib turns his attention to us once the wine is served. "Do you two plan on having children?" he asks.

"Definitely," Dex answers without hesitation. "Lots of them."

"Oh, really?" I ask, raising an eyebrow as I turn to him.

"Of course," he answers, looking at me with a straight face. "I can't wait to put a baby in her."

My back straightens, and I hold my breath as he slides his hand over my stomach, smiling at me.

"Dex, honey," I say, feeling my face get hot. "Let's not have any inappropriate touching at the dinner table," I say in a low voice.

"There's nothing inappropriate about a

husband touching his beautiful wife," Prince Kalib says, smiling as he watches Dex's hand on my stomach. Dex takes back his hand and a cold shiver shakes through me as a sense of loss settles in my belly.

I've never met a guy that I liked enough to even consider having kids with, but I decide to indulge in the fantasy a bit. It is all pretend after all.

"Would you like to start with a boy or girl?" I ask, trying to hide my smile as I look up at my pretend husband.

"It doesn't matter to me," he says, taking his napkin and placing it on his lap. "I would love to have a little boy to roughhouse with and toss around on the couch, and I would love to have a little girl to put on my shoulders and treat like a princess."

I lean toward him, trying to erase some of the vast distance between us as I picture him having a tea party with his little daughter. In my fantasy, her hair is the same color as mine.

Marv interrupts, trying to steer the conversation back to yachts, which I don't mind at all. It gives me a few minutes to envision the scenario a little more. I imagine what it would be like to be Dex's wife and have his children. He'd be frustrating as hell with his cocky attitude, but something tells me that I'd be laughing a lot in between the bouts of frustration. He's a clever guy, a talented pilot, and it's getting harder and harder to deny the physical attraction between us. Especially now that I have to look at him shirtless for most of the day.

*He's not real husband material.* I have to remind myself of that. I want to end up with a guy who will not only be good to me but who won't run out on our future kids like my dad ran out on me.

I refuse to fall for a man like that-a man who doesn't see the worth of children.

Dex seems to want kids, but I can't tell if that's part of the act or if it's for real.

"If you buy fifty-nine yachts," Marv says, speaking to the prince, "I'll throw in the sixtieth yacht for free."

"Are you okay?" Dex whispers, looking down at me.

I nod, smiling despite myself.

He takes my hand in his and gives it a gentle squeeze. *It's all part of the show*, I tell myself, even though our hands are below the table where Prince Kalib can't see them.

We keep our hands like this until the dinner arrives and we're forced to break apart so we can eat.

The staff serves fresh sushi, and for once I wish Kara was here. I would love to see how she handles raw fish in her condition. Actually, I just want to see her puke all over her perfect body.

"What can I do to make you close the deal?" Marv asks the prince. Our boss is looking pretty desperate now. He was hoping to be off this island after a quick lunch and thirty something hours later, and he hasn't made any progress.

"In my country," Prince Kalib says, lifting up his wine glass. "We don't talk business at the dinner table."

"You don't talk business anywhere," Marv mutters as his angry eyes drop to his lap.

After dinner, Prince Kalib orders us some snifters of Brandy and brings us to a large empty room with a high ceiling. It looks like a banquet hall but without any tables-just the gorgeous marble floors and the large open windows that look out onto the dark ocean.

Prince Kalib sits down at a Grand Piano in the corner and smiles as his fingers tap on the keys playfully.

"Oh, great," Marv moans behind us. "This should be horrible."

I've had one too many glasses of wine at dinner and I'm having a good time. "You should probably go check on Kara," I say, giving Marv an out.

His face lights up as he looks at me. "I should," he says, placing his drink down on the piano and straightening his sports jacket. "Excuse me, Prince Kalib. I must go attend to my sick wife."

"Of course," Prince Kalib says with a nod.

Marv shoots me a look of gratitude as he hurries out of the large room.

I'm on a private island, in one of the most gorgeous villas on the planet, with a sweet drink in my hand, the warm Caribbean breeze floating in through the open windows, about to listen to a private show beside a smoking hot pilot. I'm not about to let a cranky billionaire like Marv ruin my vibe.

"What would you like to hear?" Prince Kalib asks as he fiddles with the keys, the random tones echoing throughout the vast room.

Dex walks around the piano and whispers something in the prince's ear.

*What is he doing?*

I can't take my eyes off of him as they exchange a few hushed words. The prince nods, and Dex comes strutting over with one hand tucked behind his back and the other hand in front of him like he's offering it to me.

"Is this some kind of trap?" I ask, leaning back as I watch him with narrowed eyes.

"Can I have this dance?" he asks softly. There's no hint of sarcasm or ridicule on his face. He looks genuine as he waits for my answer with his bright blue eyes making my knees weak.

I get lost in his eyes for a moment as warm desire flutters through me. I take a deep breath, getting ready to tell him where he can shove his dance. I don't dance with my enemies; I crush them. The only time I'll dance with him is when I'm dancing on his grave.

My mind is ready to tell him that, but my hand doesn't seem to get the memo, and before I know it, I'm sliding my palm against his and stepping toward him.

*One dance won't hurt. It won't change things.*

Every nerve ending in my body is tingling like fine champagne as Dex guides me to the dance floor. He moves with the grace of a panther, and I'm worried my clumsiness is going to cramp his style.

Prince Kalib begins playing the piano softly, and I immediately recognize one of my favorite love songs: Elvis Presley's *Can't Help Falling In Love.*

"I told him this was our wedding song," he whispers as his hand slides down to my lower back. He pulls me in close with his eyes fixated on mine. My body trembles under his firm eye contact, and before I know it, we're moving around the dance floor as he takes the lead.

"I love this song," I say, looking up at his handsome face. His skin is bronzed from the sun, lighting up his gorgeous eyes in a blue fire. My eyes slowly travel down along his sharp jawline to his lips. I wonder what his lips feel like. *They look so soft.*

"I'll tell you what," Dex says as Prince Kalib starts singing softly. He's no Elvis, but he's still pretty good. "When you marry me for real, we can dance to this song."

"Marry you for real?" I say, laughing despite my face getting hot. "It's going to cost you more than a few hundred thousand dollars for me to agree to that."

"I can give you my heart," he says, holding me close. "It's all I got."

I tuck my head on his chest as we dance softly. I'm listening to the music as I contemplate his words.

"Where did you learn to dance like this?" I ask, smiling at him. "I'm impressed. You haven't stepped on my toes once."

He smiles. "I learned from the best."

"Ex-girlfriend?"

"My mother."

"Oh," I say, smiling as I picture a little Dex dancing around the living room with his mother, bumping into the coffee table as an old radio crackles out a song from the kitchen.

"She was under the belief that a real man should know how to dance with a lady."

"Your mother was right," I say, letting him spin me around. *I wonder if I'll ever meet her.*

"She loves to dance," he says, his eyes softening as he looks to the side. "My father and she were always dancing around the house every night. I used to love watching him swing her around. She would always fall into his arms, giggling at that part. When he died, my mother was so lost. She would just sit at the table and stare at the wall for hours with a blank look on her face. I tried everything to make her feel better but nothing worked. Then one day, I turned the radio on and asked her to dance. It was the first time I saw her smile, really smile, since my father passed. We danced almost every night afterward."

I let him hold me a little closer, breathing in his musky cologne as the song plays. Maybe I was wrong about him. He's actually kind of sweet.

The song ends much too early and I'm forced to let go of him.

"Thank you for the dance," I whisper, feeling empty without him in my arms.

"Anytime, Riley Coyote. Anytime."

I walk back to the piano and turn around in surprise when Dex walks in the opposite direction.

"Wonderful song," I say to the prince who is grinning proudly. "Beautiful piano playing."

"Thank you," he says, clearly touched by my words. He starts to explain how he took lessons during his time at Harvard University. I have one eye on him and one eye on Dex who's talking to one of the waiters.

Dex slips him a tip and the waiter nods, hurrying away. He snaps his fingers at two other waiters and the three of them rush out onto the beach as Dex strolls back toward us.

He slides his hand around my waist and it feels so natural that I forget to dig my nails into his forearm.

"What was that about?" I whisper to him.

"Prince Kalib," he says, ignoring my question.

"Your company has been delightful tonight, but I would love to have some alone time with my wife. Would you mind?"

He shakes his head as his fingers dance along the piano keys, playing a soft song that I don't recognize. "If I had a wife as beautiful as her, I would want to be alone with her at all times."

The sultry look he gives me makes me uncomfortable, so I step a little closer to Dex. Dex may be a creep as well, but I feel safe around him, and as much as we're at each other's throats, I know he wouldn't let anything bad happen to me.

"What are you up to?" I ask, eying him suspiciously.

"What?" he says with a shrug. "Can't a husband surprise his wife?"

"Of course," I whisper low enough that Prince Kalib can't hear. "But I'm only your pretend wife. Does that mean this is a pretend surprise and you're going to push me in the pool or something?"

He shrugs as he flashes me a sexy grin. "Meet me on the beach in ten minutes and you'll find out."

# CHAPTER THIRTEEN

*RILEY*

I sink my bare toes into the cool sand as the fire warms my face. It's beautiful. My pretend husband really outdid himself. Wherever he is.

Dex ran back inside, leaving me alone on the beach at night in front of the crackling fire. I've always wanted to have a campfire on the beach, so when Dex surprised me with one, I was really excited.

I lean back, letting my fingers slide into the powdery sand as I take turns looking from the raging fire to the diamond stars shining overhead, to the gentle waves of the dark ocean, slowly lapping up against the shore. The palms trees are keeping me company as they sway in the warm breeze, waving their palms at me like we're old friends.

I close my eyes and smile, focusing on the nice smells wafting around the beach. It smells like smoky campfire mixed with salt-water. I love it.

A delicious whiff of Dex's cologne hits my

nose, and suddenly I'm back on the dance floor, gliding around effortlessly with his strong arms wrapped around me. A dab of his cologne must have rubbed onto my skin as we played husband and wife, and now I can't stop smelling it.

It might be the fourth glass of wine I had or the heavenly scenery, but I'm beginning to enjoy my fake marital status, although it is bittersweet.

I want a husband for real, and it feels like I'll never get there. I sigh softly as I look down at the diamond ring on my finger, which is casting an orange glow from the warm fire. It's fake. It's all fake.

A thickness settles in my throat as I look up at the lonely moon in the night sky. She's been alone for ages, destined to be at the singles table forever as the stars frolic all around her. Will she ever find the love she craves so much?

I sigh as the nice mood I was in takes a sudden nosedive toward Self-Pity City. I just want a man who gets me. All of my previous boyfriends, and there haven't been many, we're all turned off by my personality. Strong, they called it as they broke up with me one by one. Exhausting. Aggressive. Bossy. Inflexible. Controlling. Too much. I've heard it all.

"You're a lot," Andy had said, looking exhausted as I sat him in the corner and made him tell me the truth. "We're supposed to be on the same side, but it feels like you're constantly against me."

I twirl the ring on my finger as I wonder if there'll ever be a wedding ring there for real. I want to get married and have a chance at the family I missed out on growing up. And I want a real man who loves me for myself, not the fake version of me that I can never keep up with.

My mind drifts back to Dex as a log shifts in the fire, sending sparks dancing up into the sky. Of all the guys I've met, Dex seems to enjoy my aggressiveness. I keep waiting for him to discover the real me and move on like all of the other guys, but the more I let him in on my destructive secret, the closer he tries to get to me. He matches me punch for punch in our sparring of words, and he seems to thrive on getting me all riled up.

My breath quickens as I picture him on the boat earlier this afternoon, refusing my demands to put on a life vest.

"If you fall overboard," I said, strapping mine on extra tight, "I'm *not* jumping over to save you."

"You're going to let me drown?" he asked, raising a questioning eyebrow at me. I can still remember how his brown hair was moving in the wind, begging me to sink my fingers into it.

"I'm warning you now," I said, crossing my arms over the thick life vest and probably looking ridiculous in the process. "I'm not drowning because of your refusal to follow basic aquatic safety rules."

"What about basic fashion rules?" he said, glancing down at the huge red vest covering half of my body. It was much too big, and my head probably looked like the tip of a hot dog wiener popping out of the bun as I stood there. "You're hiding a killer bikini behind that thing. That's just fucking cruel."

Seven minutes later, my life vest was off. He chuckled when he saw me walk by in my bikini, but he didn't say anything. Luckily for him, he didn't, or I would have shoved him over the edge of the boat.

I like to do things by the book and he doesn't. I'm not even sure if he can read.

I hold my rulebook tight. It's a comfort thing for me. He doesn't play by the rules, and he's slowly making me loosen my grip on my rulebook, which is both terribly frightening and extremely exhilarating at the same time.

*Will you stop? It's all fake.*

*This is not reality. This is a business arrangement. This is about money, not feelings.* I have to remember that before I get hurt.

But when Dex comes strolling over holding a champagne bottle in one hand and two glasses in the other, the line between reality and business gets blurred a little more.

His sports jacket is off, and he's looking so tempting with his button-up light blue shirt rolled up his thick tattooed arms. The top few buttons are open, and the wind is giving me a nice view of his hard chest.

He smiles as he plops into the white sand beside me and offers me a glass.

"You're full of surprises tonight," I say taking the champagne flute. Our fingers touch, and the tingling in my fingertips just grows with need as I pull away.

"I didn't like Prince Creep's eyes on you," he says as he pulls off the foil wrapped around the champagne bottle, exposing the cork. "I wanted you all to myself."

"Are you kidding?" I say, laughing as my gaze falls back to the fire. "He's not interested in me. He can have any girl on the planet."

"Probably," he says as he grips the cork. "But he only wants one, and he's not getting close to *my* wife."

"Fake wife," I correct.

He doesn't say anything.

I take a deep breath, enjoying his scent as he smoothly pops the cork out and holds up the smoking bottle. "Thirsty?"

"Definitely," I say, holding up my glass. He fills it with champagne and bubbles, and I can't help but smile as I look at the engagement and wedding rings on my hand next to the bubbling champagne. It looks like a wedding card.

"Was that true what you said about wanting kids in there?" I ask, taking a sip. The bubbles tickle the inside of my nose, making me smile.

"Of course," he says, looking at me with his piercing blue eyes. They have an orange glow with the fire close by, and they look even sexier than normal.

"I can't tell what's real or fake anymore," I say, looking away.

"Let me explain the difference," he says, smiling as he pours himself a glass. "When I'm talking to you, it's real. When I'm talking to the prince, it's fake."

"What about when you dance with me?" I ask. My ears heat up as I close my eyes, wishing that the wine swirling in my head hadn't let the words slip by my lips.

"That's real," he says, clinking his glass with mine. "And so is all of this."

He takes a sip of his champagne, and I watch with my heart fluttering as his sexy lips curl around the glass. My right hand slides over to my left, and I slip the wedding and engagement rings off, leaving my finger bare. I want this night to be real. No fake engagement. No fake feelings. I want to see if there's anything here for realsies.

When he's not looking, I quickly unhook the strap on my convertible bra, attach the rings to it, and clip it back into place with Kara's rings fastened securely inside of my dress.

"Do you think we'll sell any yachts?" I ask, trying to lighten the mood. My half-finished glass of champagne is getting me giddy again.

"We better," he says with a laugh. "Or Marv is going to fly us out to Mongolia and leave us there."

"Then I think we better push it a little harder."

"The fake marriage?" he asks, grinning at me. "Great idea. I could stick a baby in you for real. That would sell it."

I narrow my eyes and fight back even despite getting lightheaded all of a sudden. "You try to stick anything in me, and you'll spend the rest of the weekend in the emergency room."

He laughs softly as he refills my glass. It's different with him now. We're still at each other's throats, but it's like we're playing now and not trying to actually suffocate each other.

"I was talking about pushing the sale a little harder," I say. "It's in both of our interests for him to buy the yachts."

"It's in your *interest*," he says quickly. "You'll be off to become a pilot, and I'll be stuck here without you."

My shocked eyes dart to him. He's breathing slowly as he picks up a handful of sand, letting the grains slip through his fingers.

"Don't try to deny it," he says, looking sad as he watches the waterfall of sand fall from his hand. "I know you're going to leave once you get your money."

A heaviness settles in my chest as his words play over in my mind. I guess I always knew I would quit, but I didn't think that anyone would care. Hell, I didn't think that I would care.

Things are starting to change.

"We can still be friends," I say, nearly laughing at the ridiculousness of the statement. Me and Dex as friends. It's laughable. This is the guy who soaked me with ginger ale half an hour after I met him. He's the guy I nearly killed when he grabbed my breasts and ass without permission. This is the guy who's made me grind my teeth so much over the past few days that I might need dentures when I get home.

And what's even more laughable is that I think I might want more than to just be friends. As frustrating and cocky as he is, I'm kind of attracted to him.

"Just friends?" he asks, looking at me with a softness on his face. His eyes are asking so much more than the two words that slid out of his mouth.

I take a deep breath before vomiting out a string of arguments against why we should be anything more than friends. "We're co-workers, Dex," I say, staring at the fire but not seeing the flames as my mouth rambles on. "It's never a good idea to date people you work with. We're so different. I like safe and orderly, and you like wild and reckless. You're a bit too tall for my height. We can't stay next to each other for two minutes without arguing. You're a Leo, and I'm a Taurus. It would never work."

"So that's the con list," he says, chuckling.

"The very long con list. Now, what are the pros?"

*You're the hottest guy I've ever seen. I can't stop thinking about you. You make my body react in a way that no one else has ever done.*

"I don't know," I lie.

"Let me think of some reasons why we should be together," he says, tapping his chin as he looks up at the sky. After a few seconds, he looks at me and shrugs. "I can't think of any, but I still want to be with you."

He turns to face me and like in a trance, my body follows his. He reaches up and tucks a strand of my hair behind my ear as I get lost in his deep eyes.

He's so close. My mouth waters as his warm hand moves to my cheek and cups it, gently pulling me toward him.

*Jesus.* If my heart was a jet, it would be shattering the sound barrier right now.

His lips press softly against mine, and I lean into him, letting him take my mouth with his tongue. The world vanishes around us. There's no more crackling fire or gentle ocean. There's no more bright stars or swaying palm trees. There's only his sexy lips on mine and his silky tongue claiming my mouth.

I'm breathless when he finally pulls away, and I have to place my palm on the cool sand before I fall over. I close my eyes and take a deep breath, trying to process what just happened, but my mind is as clear as a Jackson Pollock painting.

*Did he just kiss me? Did I just like it?*

It's not fair. He looks so calm and cool as he licks his lips and reaches for the champagne bottle, refilling his glass like the world didn't just come collapsing down.

I swallow hard as I try to analyze his intentions, try to figure out his game.

Guys like him are not interested in girls like me. This is all part of our war. He's trying to make me fall for him so he can trap me like a marionette and then cut the strings that are holding me up.

"What the hell was that?" I say, wiping his sweet taste from my lips with the back of my hand. "This was not part of the deal."

He lowers his glass, turning to me with a look of confusion on his face. It's all an act. He's playing me. And I almost let him win. I almost let him get the upper hand.

"Riley, I—"

"You what?" I ask, tightening my grip on the glass in my hand. "You want to hump and dump me like all of your other girls? You want to make me have feelings for you and then hang me out to dry? Well, I'm not falling for any of that!"

"Wow," he says, shaking his head as he looks at me with sadness in his eyes.

*He's good. I'll give him that. That sadness almost looks genuine.*

I jump to my feet, pouring the rest of my champagne onto the sand. "If you try that again, I'll slap a sexual harassment suit on you so fast it will make your head spin."

"Riley," he says, looking desperate as he opens his hands. "I was just trying to—"

"I know what you were trying to do," I snap. I place the champagne flute beside him and wipe the sand off of my dress. "Don't try it again. I'm going back to the room."

I storm back to the villa with my shoulders

145

back and my chin held high, but I feel like crumbling in on myself and crying. I take one last look at Dex before I turn into the hall. He's still sitting in front of the fire, but he's abandoned his glass and is drinking straight from the bottle.

"I hope you get alcohol poisoning," I whisper before marching back to our room.

Dex comes back into the room two hours later, and I'm still awake. I'm lying on my side of the bed, feeling stupid and embarrassed about my little scene on the beach.

He made such an effort and we were actually getting along and having a connection when my insecurities came bubbling up and I freaked out.

I feel horrible. I wish I could go back in time and replay the moment after the kiss. I wouldn't have been so quick to judge. I wouldn't have been so aggressive and inflexible. I wouldn't have been 'too much,' as my ex Andy had said.

I keep my head on the pillow, staring at the wall of drawers between us as Dex lies down on the bed. He can't see me and I can't see him, but I know that he's there. I wish he would stand up and knock down the wall of drawers between us, crawl onto my side of the bed, and take my body. I want him. I need him.

I'm still not certain he's playing me, but it's worth taking a chance. It's worth it for the shot at happiness that I know is possible with Dex.

"I'm sorry," I whisper, so softly that he can't hear me. "I'm sorry I ruined the night."

I picture him on the other side with his head on the pillow, facing me like I'm facing him. I breathe softly as I drag a fingertip along the soft oak of the drawer, pretending it's his chee—

"What are you doing?"

The shock of his voice jerks me out of my haze, and I spring up to a sitting position on the mattress like Linda Blair in the Exorcist.

Dex is not lying on the other side of the wall of drawers like I had imagined. He's standing at the end of my side of the bed with a toothbrush sticking out of his smirking mouth.

"Nothing," I say, shaking my head defensively. I quickly turn from defense to offense, raising my voice as I glare at him. "What are you doing on my side of the bed anyway?"

I jump off the bed and yank my pillow under my arm. "You're spying on me, you pervert!" I shout as I struggle to rip a sheet off of the mattress. It gets stuck under the wall of drawers, and Dex chuckles as I nearly fall trying to aggressively yank it off.

"Need some help?" he asks casually as he takes the toothbrush out of his mouth.

I want to stick it in his eye.

"Not from a pervert who likes to watch me when I'm sleeping!" I yell. *Finally*. The sheet comes flying off the mattress, and I quickly wrap it up into a ball under my other arm.

"It doesn't look like you were sleeping," he says, chuckling as he watches me storm across the room. "It looks like you were longing for me and wishing that I would give you another kis—"

"I *was* sleeping!" I shout, trying to block out his words.

"You were doing something," he says, giving me a frustrating grin, "but it wasn't sleepi—"

I slam the bathroom door closed and lock myself inside. My ears are burning with embarrassment as I lie on the cold tiles for the second night in a row.

My first week on the job is going just fucking great.

# CHAPTER FOURTEEN

## *DEX*

I guess it's no surprise that Riley avoids me all morning.

She's gone when I wake up, and she doesn't show up at the dining room for breakfast. I rub my eyes as I have my first sip of coffee. I barely slept last night. I kept tossing and turning, thinking about that kiss.

My cock was rock hard as I kept picturing how soft her lips were, the feel of her hands on my chest, the sound of the little whimper that escaped from her throat when I pulled away. I spent hours trying to remember every detail of the moment from the roaring fire beside us to the way my heart was hammering in my chest.

It was perfect.

And then it all went to hell.

I'm still shaking my head over what happened. One minute she's leaning into my kiss, sliding her sweet tongue across mine, moaning as I take her mouth, and then in one beat of a pounding heart, she snaps, yelling out accusations that I'm trying to play her and threatening me with a sexual harassment suit. I'm not worried about that one. Even if she tries to sue me, the judge will take one look at her beautiful face and smoking hot body and let me off the hook. Anyone who takes one look at her would know that I had no choice in the matter. How could I not sexually harass a girl like her?

"Where's the wife?" Kara asks, smirking at me as she sits down at the table with a single slice of watermelon on her plate. That's all she's eating for breakfast.

"I don't know," I say, trying not to glance at her chest, but it's hard with the way that she's pressing her big tits together for me.

"Maybe she's in *my* room," she says, licking a finger, and then sliding it down her chest. "Want me to go help you find her?"

I glance over at Marv who's bossing the breakfast chef around, yelling something about how omelets should have bacon in them. I must admit, he's making some good points.

"So, I guess you're feeling better?" I ask, grinning as she looks away in embarrassment. "Maybe if you eat a little more than a watermelon slice for breakfast your stomach can handle some more action."

"There's only one type of action that I'm interested in," she says, giving me fuck-me eyes as she takes the pink piece of fruit and licks it from the bottom to the top without ever breaking eye contact.

"Mmmmmm," she moans as she slides it

between her glossy lips, sucking on it like a cock.

"You should have gotten a banana," I say, peeling my eyes off her as I stand up. "It would have made a better visual."

"I like it *juicy*," she says, licking her fingers. "Our deal is still on, Dex. Why is she still here?"

I've suddenly lost my appetite as guilt takes my hunger's place and makes my stomach harden. I should never have made that deal with her, and I'm about to tell her that when Marv walks over, huffing and puffing like the big bad wolf.

"Can you believe this guy?" he asks with his shoulders tight. "He only put *vegetables* in my omelet!"

"The bastard," I say, getting up from the table. I down my coffee and look at Kara. "I can find my wife by myself, thanks."

"Your loss," she says as I leave the room. I would have jumped at the chance to be alone with the stunning Hidden Pleasures model a few days ago, but I'm a married man now, even though my wife hates me and she refuses to give me any action. Yup, it certainly feels like I'm a married man.

I walk around the monstrous villa looking everywhere for Riley but I can't find her anywhere. After I pass the twentieth expensive-looking painting, I walk outside, exploring the north side of the island. The waves are fierce up here, and I'm tempted to grab a surfboard and head into the water.

That idea quickly drains as the prince comes walking out of the ocean with a surfboard tucked under his arm.

"Good morning, Dex," he says, waving to me as he approaches.

*Shit.* This is the last person I want to talk to.

"Did you think about my offer?" he asks, shaking the water out of his hair.

The look I give him makes him take a step back. "With all due respect, Dex," he says, choosing his words carefully. "We're both men who love women. So, let's put any petty jealousy aside and do what we do best, enjoy the beautiful women at our disposal."

At our disposal. He makes them sound like fucking ice cream cones. Lick 'em and toss them aside when you're done. But I guess I should expect that from a man who has a harem of sixty women at *his* disposal.

"Sixty of the most beautiful women on the planet," he says, his eyes pleading with me. "All on their knees for you. What do you say?"

I step forward, gritting my teeth as I picture holding his head under the water until he sinks to the bottom of the ocean where he belongs.

"You can stick your offer up your royal ass," I say, slowly spitting out every word. "With all due respect."

"That's too bad," he says, looking disappointed. "Riley is quite the woman. I would have enjoyed having her warm my bed."

*Yeah, so would I.*

I've had enough of this guy talking that way about my girl. Riley may not know it yet, but she's *my* girl.

"If I ever hear you speak about my wife in that way again," I say, glaring at him with cold hard eyes. My legs are planted in a fighting stance and my chest is thrust out like an alpha gorilla defending his territory. "I'll rip your tongue out of your mouth."

He lets out a heavy sigh as he walks over to the little hut and places his surfboard on the rack with the others. "I was afraid you were going to respond like that," he says, running a hand through his wet hair. "But please. I beg you to reconsider."

He points to a cluster of palm trees with a stone path snaking through them. "You should head down that path before you make your decision final," he says. The way he's smiling makes me think it's a trap. "Truly see what you'll be missing."

Without another word, he grabs his towel and walks away, leaving me staring at the turbulent waves that are crashing onto the rocky shore.

I glance over at the path when he's gone, wondering what is up there. After a minute, curiosity gets the better of me, and I'm quickly walking down the path. It takes about fifteen minutes of walking through tropical bush before I'm out on the other side of the island.

*Oh.*

I stop mid-stride when I see what the prince was talking about. I'm on top of a hill looking over a white sand beach on the north west-side of the island. There is a cluster of villas to my left, but I don't even give them so much as a glance from my spot on the path because to the right are sixty stunning women frolicking in the sand. Most don't have their bikini tops on, some have nothing on, but they're all gorgeous.

*So, this is where he hides them.*

This is where the harem lives. They have villas, inground pools, a white sand beach with calm turquoise water, and a bar with unlimited drinks.

As I'm staring at a spectacular set of tits from

a girl on the beach volleyball court, the magnitude of what Prince Kalib is offering hits me like a kick to my nuts.

Sixty women.

How can I turn that down?

*By turning around and walking back down the path.*

I listen to the voice inside my head for a change and run down the path before my other head makes me turn around and introduce myself to the ladies.

My frustration grows with every slap of my flip flops on the path. My chest is tight, my head is starting to ache, and I want to punch down a palm tree.

I don't understand why this is happening, why I'm turning down this amazing opportunity.

But I know the answer. *It's because of Riley.*

I don't even like her, and she fucking hates me. So why is she the only thing I can think about?

Every time I consider going down to the beach to meet the ladies, I see her disapproving face, and it makes me sick to my stomach.

I've wanted to sleep with her since the moment I saw her, but this is different. This is getting beyond lust. I told her about dancing with my mother, and I've never told anyone that.

*Jesus fucking Christ.*

Am I falling in love with her?

I'm still amped up when I decide to take the

plane out to blow off some steam. Flying planes always helps me focus and usually helps me work through a problem.

And believe me, falling in love with Riley is definitely a problem.

I was hoping to have a friends with benefits type of relationship with her when we first met, but this, this was never in the plans.

"There's my girl," I whisper when I see the plane parked on the beach where I left it. It's tied to two stakes dug into the white sand.

All of the stress, worry, and anxiety that I've been feeling in the past half hour just drift away with the breeze when I see my other girl inside the plane.

Riley is sitting in the pilot's seat, looking more beautiful than ever. Her brown hair is finally tamed under the headset as she looks over the checklist card. Her succulent lips are moving as she reads, her hands hovering over the instrument panel, pretending to push buttons and flick switches.

She's so focused on what she's doing that she doesn't notice me approaching. It doesn't help that I'm sneaking over, hoping to scare her.

"Ahh!" she screams when I knock on the window, popping up out of nowhere.

She turns to me with a scowl on her face as she clutches her chest, her heart probably pounding away. "What?" she snaps, not even bothering to open the window.

Something tells me that if she had a pilot's license, she would be taking off right now, desperate to get away from me.

"Are you stealing my plane?"

She huffs out a breath and then rolls her eyes

before rolling down the window. "I was just practicing the safety checks."

"It's against FAA regulations to sit in a Captain's seat without a licensed pilot observing," I say, pulling a Riley and throwing the rulebook in her face.

"You're right. I'm sorry," she says, turning red as she unbuckles her seatbelt. "I shouldn't be here."

She tries to open the door, but I hold it closed.

"It's okay," I say, giving her a real smile. I was just trying to bug her. I didn't want her to actually feel bad. "I'm a licensed pilot and I'm observing. Pretend like I'm not here."

"That's impossible," she says, her adorable little ears turning red as she looks down in her lap. "Especially after the disaster last night."

"Disaster?" I say, jerking my head back. Does she think that kissing me was a disaster? "I had a great time last night."

"You did?" she asks, turning to me with raised eyebrows.

I nod. "Didn't you?"

She takes a deep breath, looking too uncomfortable to answer. I decide to save her and change the subject. I know she had a good time no matter what she thinks she thinks.

"You really like planes, don't you?" I say, peeking past her to the notes on the passenger's seat. There are at least six notebooks packed with multi-colored post-it notes sticking out everywhere.

The redness in her face starts to disappear as she looks at me with excited eyes. "I *love* planes. I've been wanting to be a pilot since I was old enough to point at the planes in the sky."

"Have you had any training?"

"No," she says, shaking her head. "I mean, I'm self-taught. I've read every pilot textbook about ten times each, and I've clocked over three hundred hours on my flight simulator on my computer, but that's it."

"That's it?" I ask with a chuckle. "Shit, that's more than most graduates have done."

"Yeah, but they've actually flown a plane," she says, looking down at the yoke in her hands. "I haven't."

"So, let's go," I say, slapping the side of the plane. "The keys are under the seat."

She looks so shocked as I duck under the wing and walk around the back to the passenger's side, untying the ropes as I go. Her mouth is hanging open as I open the door and slip inside.

"We *can't!*" she says, swallowing hard as she looks around. "This is against so many regulations. It's breaking rules, and laws!"

"That's what makes it so good," I say, grinning at her.

But she refuses. She may have loosened up a little since she met me, but she still has a long way to go before she's breaking laws by flying airplanes without a license. We'll get there one day.

After a few minutes of arguing, I'm in the pilot's seat and she's in the passenger's seat watching.

"Okay," I say through the headsets. "Tell me what to do."

She's gripping the laminated checklist so hard that it's bending under her fingertips. "Check that the circuit breakers are in."

I nod. "Check it."

She does and then looks at the shaking checklist in her hands, although I don't think she even needs it. She probably has every item memorized. "Make sure the avionics power switch is off."

"Is it?"

She nods. She has a smile on her face that cannot be contained as she bounces her knee up and down with excitement. "Yes."

I watch her as she goes over the checklist, making sure everything is ready before I start the engine. When it is, I jump out of the plane and push it into the water, jumping back in before it floats away without me.

I let her start the engine, and she looks thrilled as the propeller starts spinning.

She watches me like a hawk as I taxi the plane out into the open water, and I watch her like a hawk when she reaches into the back to grab the GPS off the back seat. *Fuck, she's hot.*

Ten minutes later, we're in the sky, circling around Prince Kalib's private island and heading out to sea.

"Should we just leave and never come back?" I ask through the headsets when the island is safely behind us.

Her little laugh gets my heart pumping. "I hate Kara, and Marv is no treasure, but even I wouldn't do that to them. They all look so miserable there."

"They're miserable everywhere." Wait until she sees how much Kara likes Mongolia. I decide to not ruin the moment by bringing that up.

She married him for his money and he

married her because she was the only Hidden Pleasures model who would talk to him. They're not exactly a model of a happy marriage.

"How's our altitude?" I ask, changing the subject to something that will get a smile on her beautiful face.

She leans over me to take a look at the instrument panel. The fruity smell of her hair is making my heart pound as fast as the engine.

"Low," she says with her gorgeous face wrinkled up in concentration.

"How do we fix it?"

"Pull the yoke up," she says, looking like she's loving every minute of this. If I'm being honest, so am I.

"You do it."

"I can't," she says, looking at me with confusion in her bright green eyes.

"Why not?"

"Because I can't reach it."

I hold the yoke with my left hand and tap my thigh with my right. "Come on over," I say, trying to hide my grin. "You're driving."

Her face reddens as she looks down at my legs. "Where do I sit?"

"On my lap."

She bites her bottom lip as she thinks about it, and the sight is so sexy that I'm glad she's not on me already or else she would be feeling my parking brake against her ass.

"That would be inappropriate." She has barely taken a breath since I brought it up.

"We're already way beyond inappropriate," I say, tapping my lap again. "You want to fly a plane or not?"

After a few seconds of hesitation, she takes off her seatbelt and is climbing over. *I can't believe that actually worked.*

I hold my breath as she straddles me in a reverse cowgirl, lowering her perfect ass onto my lap. Her soft brown hair tickles my face as she takes control of the airplane and I try to take control of my excited body. *Don't get a boner. Don't get a boner.*

She'll insist on riding home in the back seat if she feels me go hard against her, and I want to keep her right where she is.

I'm so distracted by the beautiful curve of her ass on me and my heart that's pounding furiously in my chest that I completely forget about flying the plane. Luckily, she knows what she's doing.

Riley is smiling wide as she holds onto the yoke, steering the plane perfectly. "This is incredible," she gasps as she dips left then right, testing out the controls. "I'm actually flying! I can't believe it!"

"You're actually sitting on my lap," I answer. "I can't believe *that!*"

"Shut up!" she says, playfully swatting me. "Even you can't ruin this moment for me."

"I wouldn't want to." She smiles as I rest my chin on her shoulder, watching the gorgeous Caribbean scenery in front of us.

"Can I go higher?" she asks, turning to me with a beautiful smile on her face.

"You're the pilot," I answer. "You can go wherever you want to."

A second later, she hits full power without me having to tell her, and she tilts the plane. I swallow a groan as her round ass presses ever harder against me as the plane climbs into the air. "Good," I say in a raspy voice when we straighten back out, high above the clouds now. "Did you check your—"

"Airspeed? Yup."

She's good. As much as I would hate to admit it, she would make an excellent pilot. Her attention to detail, insistence on following every single rule, and quick reaction speed are all excellent traits for a pilot to have.

We spend the next hour flying around like this with her on my lap. She's enjoying finally getting to fly an airplane, and I'm enjoying finally getting to touch her ass without getting smacked.

"I think it's time to turn back," I say when I look at the fuel gauge.

"So soon?" she asks, looking disappointed as she looks at me over her shoulder.

"We're getting low on fuel," I say. "And my legs have been asleep for the past twenty minutes."

"Oops!" she says, trying to climb off me. "I'm sorry."

"Don't be," I say, holding her in place. I'm not ready for her to leave.

She's turned in an awkward angle, her face hovering over mine. I take the yoke with my left hand and hold the plane steady as our eyes connect, heated desire passing between us. Her lips part as her face goes still and her cheeks turn an adorable shade of pink.

Our eyes are locked on each other like we're hypnotized and unable to look away. My hand drifts up to her neck, and I cradle the back as I gently pull her toward me. She offers no resistance except for a little moan as our lips come together once again.

We're kissing with a greed and hunger that was missing last night. Her hands are all over me, grabbing and pulling as I position her back on my lap. She straddles me as she cups my cheeks and plunges her tongue down my throat.

I'm so hard. She starts grinding against me, and it's pure fucking torture, but I have to pull my mouth away from hers to make sure the plane isn't flying upside down. After a quick check of the instrument panel, our mouths come back together in a desperate crush of lips.

Our tongues are tangled as our bodies melt into each other. I have one hand on the yoke and the other is clumsily trying to undo the buttons of her shirt. She smacks my hand away as she pulls her mouth away from mine, her lips and mouth red from my scratchy beard.

She looks at me with pure lust on her face as she quickly undoes her buttons, staring at me under her lush, dark lashes.

I take one last glimpse at the instrument panel as she undoes the last button of her shirt. She rips it open, and the sight of her on my lap with only a white lacy bra covering her tits is enough to make my dick ache with need.

She grinds her jean-covered pussy on my erection as my mouth devours the tops of her breasts. I tug her bra down and groan as I take a hard, pink nipple into my mouth, swirling my tongue around it. Her tits are even more perfect than I had imagined, and I suck, lick, and nibble them until her eyes are closed and she's panting like she's about to come.

The soft noises she's making through my headset are driving me crazy, making me forget all about reality-which is not a good thing when you're flying a plane.

She reaches down and is desperately trying to unbutton my shorts, but there's more body than room in the small plane, and she can't maneuver in a way that gives her access. I grab her hips and try to move her so I can unbutton my shorts but when I do, she leans back and hits the yoke.

My stomach flies up to my throat as the ground falls from under us and we plummet.

"SHIT!" I shout as she flies off of me, slamming into the windshield with a thud. She screams as she looks back at the view behind her which is all ocean as we nosedive toward the water like a missile.

My heart is going so fast that it's about to explode as I try to regain control of the plane. We start spinning as the plane engine stalls, and no matter what I try, I can't get it started again.

I gulp as I look at Riley who is plastered against the windshield, screaming like a madwoman. The ocean behind her is getting really close, really fast.

*At least I get to stare at those beautiful tits as I die.*

# CHAPTER FIFTEEN

## *RILEY*

I'm going to die. With my tits out, no less.

My stomach is in my throat as we plummet to the water. With the back of my head plastered to the windshield, I can't see where we're headed, but I imagine it's blue and deep and scary as hell. And from the look on Dex's face, I'd guess that we're going to arrive any second now.

He grabs my belt buckle with one hand and yanks me into my seat.

"Buckle up, buttercup," he says, holding me against the seat as he struggles to break out of the nosedive. My fingers feel as nimble as cinder blocks as I try to fasten my seatbelt. I finally get it clipped in without a second to spare because Dex releases me to flick a couple of switches on the flight deck.

*My God.*

The ocean is approaching so fast. I'm hyperventilating as I wonder if we'll explode on impact at this speed or just rocket down to the bottom of the ocean where our heads will explode from the pressure.

I try to say a last prayer, one to each of the Gods just to hedge my bets, but I can't speak. My chest is burning, and it feels like my voice is being shoved down to my stomach.

Dex's flexed forearms strain as he pulls the yoke up, starting to straighten the plane out. He flicks a few switches, yanks open the throttle and thankfully, the engine starts back up. The propeller roars back to life, and in the next few seconds, Dex has the plane level and flying parallel to the ground.

Neither of us says anything for at least a minute. I'm the one to break the silence when he turns over and takes a long look at my breasts.

"Can you keep your eyes on the clouds?" I ask, yanking my shirt closed.

"I was keeping my eyes on heaven," he says, smiling to himself. I'm not in the mood.

"Are you seriously talking about sex?" I say, my voice just an octave under a scream. "We almost died!"

"No, we didn't," he says, adjusting his shorts in his crotch region. My arousal is somewhere back up there at ten thousand feet, but he's still as hard as when I was grinding on him. *Shit. I was grinding on him.*

*How does he keep getting my body to do that so easily?*

"I'm an Air Force pilot," he says in that smug cocky voice that drives me nuts. "I've done more than this."

"This is not an F-22 Raptor," I scream, my blood pressure jacking back up again. "It's a prop plane. It can't do stunts."

"I just did it," he says with a shrug.

"And you got kicked out of the Air Force, hot shot," I say. It's a low blow, and we both know it. His knuckles turn white as he squeezes the yoke, his jaw clenched shut as he stares at the horizon.

I take a deep breath, feeling bad as I look over at him. It was my big ass that hit the yoke and made us free fall after all.

"Dex," I say softly after a few minutes of silence. "I'm really sor—"

He flicks the switch to my microphone off before I can finish.

*Fine, asshole. I'm not sorry.*

We ride the rest of the way back to the island in silence.

"Dex," I say when we're back on the beach. "Are you not going to talk to me anymore?"

He slams the metal stakes that the plane is attached to into the sand with a little more force than necessary. I cringe as he picks up the hammer and smashes it down onto the stake, grunting as he's probably picturing my face on the head of it.

His body is tense as he moves around with short jerky movements. He looks pissed.

And it's my fault. Just as we were starting to get along...

"I'm sorry," I say, feeling a lump in my throat. "I didn't mean it. My adrenaline was going and I—"

"Do you want to know why I got kicked out

of the Air Force?" he asks, waving the hammer around. He stops when he sees it still in his grip and tosses it onto the sand. "Since you're always bringing it up."

"I'm sorry, Dex," I say again, feeling horrible. He made a dream of mine come true today, and I ruined it all. He didn't deserve that. He doesn't deserve any of the ways that I've been treating him. "You don't have to tell me anything."

He exhales hard as he places his hands on his hips, staring down at the sand. A bead of sweat drips down his temple as he closes his eyes. "It wasn't because I messed up," he says, running his hand through his hair. "And it wasn't because I was incompetent or negligent."

He opens his eyes and looks at me with a sadness that breaks my heart. "I got kicked out because I disobeyed a direct command."

"You don't have to tell me," I say, feeling terrible that I'm making him tell me his secret.

"I want to tell you," he says, locking eyes on me. "I want you to know."

My body goes still as I wait for it, my hands trembling by my sides.

"I was doing a tour in Iraq," he says with a hard swallow. His eyes are suddenly off the beach and back in the war-torn country. I don't like this. I wish he was back here with me.

"I was flying the Raptor on a mission," he says, his voice thick with emotion. "There was a known high-ranking terrorist in a house, and I was on my way over there. Yazen Maalouf. It had been confirmed that he was in the location, meeting with his mistress. My orders were to take the house down, but when I was approaching with my finger on the trigger, I saw two kids playing in the front yard."

I get a slight chill despite the warm sun on my face as I listen to him. I can't imagine what that would feel like-being ordered to kill children.

"The heartless fuck on the other line of the radio was screaming at me to fire, but I couldn't. I kept looking at the kids. My finger wouldn't move. They were smiling as they pointed up at my jet, and I just couldn't. I flew by and Yazen Maalouf got away."

I want to run to him and feel his strong arms wrap around me, but I just stand there, standing awkwardly and quiet.

"That's how I got dishonorably discharged," he says with a sigh. "I'm lucky I didn't have to face the firing squad."

"You did the right thing." My thoughts are jumbled right now but I know it. He did the right thing.

"Did I?" he asks, looking at me with sad eyes. "Three days later, Yazen Maalouf was responsible for an attack that killed two of my fellow soldiers. Ask their wives and children if I did the right thing."

"Dex," I say, breathless. "That's not your fault. Those soldiers signed up to the military, knowing their deaths were a possibility. Those kids had no choice in the matter. They were innocent."

"Maybe," he says as he pulls out his sunglasses and puts them on. "Or maybe I deserve to face the firing squad."

"Dex," I say as he walks away. It falls on deaf ears.

I've been so busy thinking that Dex and I have been fighting a war that I forgot he really did fight in one. It couldn't have been an easy decision what he did, but I think he made the right choice.

I'm lost in thought, feeling horrible at all the wrong turns the day took that I don't notice Kara walking up to me.

"You two are getting close," she says, eying me savagely. "I don't like it."

"I don't really care," I spit back at her. My eyes fall to the hammer in the sand and I'm tempted. Man, am I tempted.

"First you flirt with my husband," she says, twirling a circle with her finger in her perfect blonde hair. "Now you're flirting with my pilot. Are you trying to annoy me, or are you just a really big whore?"

I step up to her but then swallow my words when I remember what's on the line. I have a big payday coming my way if I can get the prince to purchase the yachts and then I can finally pay my way through flight school.

But that's not what's really getting to me. If I get fired, I'll probably never see Dex again, and as much as I hate to admit it, that's the thing that's really going to hurt.

"I'm sorry you feel that way, Mrs. Gladstone," I say, lowering my head in a show of submission. It kills me to do it, but now is not the time. One day it will be, but not right now.

"Keep your stinky truck-stop pussy where it belongs, in your pants," she says, glaring at me. Her glare turns into a smile as she raises her chin in triumph. "If I see you speak to Dex one more time. I'm getting you fired."

This day has just gone from bad to worse.

And the sun is still up. I still have a few hours to go.

# CHAPTER SIXTEEN

*RILEY*

I skip dinner and find a secluded spot where I can be alone and think. Both Prince Kalib and Marv are expecting me, and I'll probably get fired for this, but right now I don't really care. I can't face Dex.

It's a beautiful night, and instead of facing the man who is constantly on my mind, I'm playing it safe and hiding like a scared little kid. I wandered around the resort until I came across an inground pool behind a small private villa, the kind of place where a couple comes to escape for a weekend. It's tucked away off the path, hidden by palm trees, tall bushes, and the dark night sky. It's perfect. Just what I need.

I can't stop thinking of this afternoon and how I messed everything up. I thought I hated Dex, but the truth is a little more complicated than that.

I can't deny any longer how my body reacts so strongly to him. It's crazy how he can turn me into a sex-crazed she-beast so easily. Just the lightest touch from him can leave me so flustered. I wasn't planning on kissing him or doing anything else today, but when I was sitting on his lap in the plane, I couldn't help myself. His warm breath was tickling the back of my neck as his strong arms wrapped around me. It felt so perfect sitting on his lap as I flew the plane, enjoying the feeling of his big package resting against my ass.

When I turned and we were within kissing distance, it felt like my body was no longer mine. It was all his, under his complete control. The kiss was incredible, unlike anything I've ever felt before, and I just had to go further.

There's something there. As frustrating and soul-crushing as it is to admit, there's something there.

I see him everywhere and in everything. The bright turquoise water of the lit-up pool reminds me of his eyes, the gentle swooshing of the breeze reminds me of his breath when we're nice and close, and the long pool noodle floating in the water reminds me of his long, hard-well, you get the idea.

He's like a drug.

If God made crack into a human form, he'd be named Dex. But God couldn't be this cruel. This has the devil's work written all over it.

Dex is pure sin.

Sinfully hot, sinfully tempting, sinfully sexy.

Definitely the work of the devil.

So how come when he smiles at me it always feels like I'm in heaven?

After another half an hour of stewing in my own guilt and self-pity, the devil himself arrives dressed in jeans and a tight black shirt. Dex is wandering down the path with his hands in his pockets and his shoulders slumped forward. His chest looks massive as it strains against the tight material, and his tattooed arms look more jacked than usual. *He must have hit the gym before dinner.* He's wearing a matching black hat that's pulled down low over his eyes, giving him a dark look that I really like.

I'm sitting in the shadows and Dex doesn't see me. I can just hide here and admire him, letting him walk by without saying a word, but we all know that's not going to happen.

I'm usually so in control. In control of my desires, my thoughts, my emotions, my body. But when Dex comes around they're all over the place. I'm a hot mess of desire, my thoughts are dominated by him, my emotions feel like a roller coaster, and my body betrays me with every look he gives me.

Eight billion people on the planet, and my heart has chosen him. I can't help but wonder if my brain was consulted before the decision was made. I highly doubt it.

"Dex," I whisper just loud enough for him to hear.

He turns, and after a few seconds of searching, his eyes settle on me, sending warm shivers cascading through my body. His face is still and calm, but his eyes are wild and alive, saying all the things he can't or won't say.

"Hey, Riley," he says quietly. My breath catches in my throat. I love hearing my name on his lips. I've heard people call me by name for decades, but no one can make it sound as special as Dex does. "Would you like some company?"

I swallow hard as I nod. He comes over and sits on my lounge chair even though there's an empty one beside me. He looks so gorgeous, and I'm suddenly wishing I chose something to wear that was a little sexier than black yoga pants and a long white tank top.

"How was dinner?" I ask, trying to break the silence. I don't really care about the dinner. I'm just hoping he has forgiven me for my outburst this afternoon.

"Not the same without you," he says, exhaling as he shakes his head. "I forgot how boring things are when you're not around."

I chuckle, smiling back at him. "You definitely make things interesting as well."

"I'll take that as a compliment," he says, smiling as he looks down at his hand.

It's going better than I thought it would, but there's still something nagging at me. "Are you mad at me?" I ask, just having to get it out there.

He jerks his head up and looks at me with confusion in his narrowed eyes. "Aren't you mad at me?"

"I don't even know anymore," I say with a laugh.

He takes my hand and smiles. "Me neither. I guess that's something we're going to have to get used to."

"What do you mean?" I ask, enjoying the feeling of his skin on mine.

"We're going to end up together." He says it like it's an undebatable fact. "And sometimes it's going to be hard with us," he says, gently sliding his fingertips over my wrist and giving me goosebumps. "I have a feeling we're going to butt heads a lot and be at each other's throats, and even we won't know why. Sometimes it may feel like it can't possibly work. Sometimes it may feel like we're over. But I want you to know that it never will be. We're going to have a long story, you and me. And it won't end. Ever. I promise you that."

"How can you say that?" I ask. "We just met." But I know he's right. My heart is racing from just a whiff of his cologne. My skin is tingling from only his nearby presence.

"Because I can't stop fucking thinking about you," he says, exhaling hard. "I can't have a thought without you in it. That's how I know."

I could say the same thing about him, but I don't. Because I'm afraid. He's wild and reckless. He's the opposite of the safe choice and that scares me.

I don't want it to but it does.

"It's okay if you don't feel the same," he says, cupping my cheek and gently caressing it with his thumb. His eyes are so bright. He's so beautiful. "You will one day. I'll make sure of that."

"Maybe," I say, letting myself enjoy the fantasy of it for a minute until reality comes crashing down. "You're saying that now, but if we make love, what then? You're going to lose interest."

"This is not just about sex," he says, locking eyes on me. The seriousness of his look gives me shivers. "If this was about sex, I'd be on the other side of the island right now."

I tilt my head, wondering what he's talking about, but he doesn't explain.

"I've never met a girl like you before," he says, making me lightheaded. "You stand up to me. You call me on my bullshit. You make me laugh. You're smart and funny, and believe me, you are the most beautiful woman I've ever seen."

I don't know how to explain how he makes me feel, but that's why lips were invented. To say the things that words can't.

I take his hand and lean in, smiling as I press my lips to his. It's a soft sweet kiss, but something tells me it's just an appetizer and I'm going to be feasting all night.

His look is full of heated desire when I pull away. His grip tightens on my wrist as his breathing becomes shallow and strained, like he's holding himself back.

I don't want him to hold back anymore. My body aches for him.

"I can give you what you want." His voice is deep and raspy. His look is hungry and full of lust. "I can give you what you *crave*. Come on, Riley Coyote, let me give it to you."

His words and voice and smell are all working together to make me lose control. I want him to be mine. I want him to rip off my clothes and make me his.

But I want more than just his body. What I crave is not just the physical. I want all of him. His mind, body, and soul. I want *him*.

"You couldn't give me what I crave," I gasp. My voice is so scratchy. My breath is so ragged. How does he do this to me so easily?

"I can do anything for you," he whispers as he slides his fingers into my hair. "I can be anyone for you."

I grab his wrist and hold it in place as I stare into his eyes. "I don't want you to be anything for me," I say to him. "I just want you to be *with* me."

He kisses me with a passion that I'm not prepared for but is a welcome surprise. He devours my mouth, kissing me in a way that I've never been kissed before.

Our hands are everywhere, sliding under clothes and over soft skin, pulling each other closer. I take off his hat and run my fingers through his messy hair, loving the way it looks. My palm falls on his chest, and I smile when I feel his heart hammering as hard as mine.

Arousal swirls through me and settles between my legs. It's then that I know we're going to go all the way. It's then that I know I couldn't stop myself even if I wanted to.

"Tell me what you see when you picture it," he whispers in my ear as he slides his hand up my stomach. "Am I sliding in and out of you nice and slow? Or are you bent over like a yoga master screaming as I fuck you like a sweaty jackhammer?"

I gulp when his hand pulls down my bra and grabs a hold of my breast, massaging it with his strong grip. The warmth between my legs is turning into a fire with his words. It's turning into an inferno under his touch.

"It's the second one, isn't it?" he groans into my ear. "Hot. Wild. Rough sex. Test how far back your legs can go sex. See how soundproof the walls are sex. Is that what you think about?"

I can barely talk. My voice is gone. The only noise I can make is the pounding of my heart and the ragged breaths coming out of my wet parted lips.

"Dex…"

He kisses my neck as he releases my breast and runs his hand up my inner thigh. "Is that what you fantasize about? Is that what you want?"

I nod. It's all I ever want when he's around.

"Is that what you think about when you touch yourself through those lacy yellow panties?" he asks, his hands finally reaching my wet pussy.

"Yes…" I gasp, throwing my head back as he glides his fingers over my sex. My wetness is soaking through my underwear, soaking through my pants. I want to take them off. I want to take everything off until it's just our bodies touching with nothing getting in the way.

"I want you to fuck me, Dex," I moan as his fingertip finds my throbbing clit and rubs it in little circles. I would laugh if I wasn't already so far gone. *I want you to fuck me, Dex.* Those words shouldn't go together, but right now they feel perfectly fucking right as they roll off my tongue.

My pants are the first to go. Then his shirt and then mine.

I moan when he stands up and I see the long rod pressing out against the inside of his jeans. I bite my bottom lip in anticipation as he unbuckles his belt and slides them down his muscular legs. His hard cock looks huge as it fights the tight material of his white boxer briefs. I lean forward, wanting to set it free.

Every inch of him from the neck down is covered in hard sexy muscle. If it wasn't for the incessant throbbing between my legs I would stare at him for hours. But there will be time for that later. Right now, I just want him in me.

He steps back to the beach chair, but instead of sitting down like I expect, he slides his arms under me and picks me up, cradling me to his chest.

"Was that our first fight?" he asks between kisses.

I smile. "The first of many. Is it bad that our first time having sex is going to be make-up sex?"

He shakes his head as he smiles at me. "We have three of the best kinds of sex combined. It's going to be epic."

I look up at him and smile as my hand slides over his hard, naked chest. "Three of the best kinds of sex?"

"First time sex," he says, giving me a soft kiss on the lips. "Make-up sex," he says, kissing me again.

"And the third?"

He turns around and walks to the pool, carrying me as easily as if I was made of rose petals. "In the pool at night sex," he answers with a grin. "It's the best."

"I didn't bring my bathing suit," I say, giving him a smirk as he walks down the steps into the water.

"Perfect."

He crushes his lips to mine as he walks into the pool, carrying me into the warm inviting water. I moan into his mouth when I feel his hard-on press up against my outer thigh. He's holding me so tight, his arms wrapped possessively around me, pulling me as close as possible to him.

The warm water creeps up to Dex's waist and then he dips down and it's up to our necks. We're still kissing like the only air we can get is from each other.

"Take off your clothes for me, Riley Coyote," he commands in his deep gravelly voice.

I swallow hard as I step out of his protective embrace and reach behind my back. Any shyness I usually have is gone. I want him to see. I want him to see everything.

His hungry eyes widen as I slide my bra down my arms, letting my breasts fall free. The water is up to my shoulders but that's not good enough for him.

"Stand up," he commands, keeping his heated eyes locked on my body.

I do as he says and stand up, showing him everything. My knees are weak. My heart is pounding in my chest. My nipples harden to the point of pain as he stares at them with that dark hungry look.

"Take off your panties," he demands. His voice is tight with pleasure as he growls out his command.

There's no question he's in control of my body. I'm a slave to his words.

I hook two fingers into my panties and am about to pull them down when he stops me. "Wait. Turn around."

My heart is pounding nervously as I turn away from him, staring at the empty chair with our clothes piled on it.

"Now arch your back and slowly pull your panties down."

I'm usually so shy to get naked in front of men, but with Dex I'm enjoying the thrill. I take a deep breath and hold it in as I slide my underwear over the curve of my ass and down my legs, enjoying the tingling rush of adrenaline at being so exposed for him.

"Beautiful," his voice purrs as I step out of my panties and let them float away. "Now bend over, grab your ass cheeks and spread them for me."

I'm panting and trembling as I do what he

says, gripping my cheeks and pulling them apart for him. He growls in approval behind me.

He moves through the water like a shark and suddenly his strong hands are on me, bending me over as he replaces my hands with his own. He lets out a low groan as he spreads my legs and stares at my sex that's throbbing with need.

A slow soft lick has my legs buckling, but his arm is there, tightening around my waist and holding me up as he licks me again.

I cry out his name as his tongue finds my aching clit, and he sucks it. We're outside in the open, and if anyone walks by they'll see me bent over in the water with Dex behind me with his face buried between my legs, but I don't care. I can't focus on that right now, not with Dex's hot tongue sliding between my folds. His beard is scratchy on my soft inner thigh as he plunges his tongue into my hole, making me shudder.

He picks up the pace, holding me tight as he eats me out from behind. My hands reach out to grip something, anything, but only hit water.

The sensation is so fucking intense. I'd sink to the bottom if he wasn't holding me up.

He flicks his tongue on my clit and then slips two fingers inside me, groaning as he rubs my sweet spot. "I just had to taste you." He squeezes my waist as he dips his head back down. "And fuck, Riley, you taste delicious."

My jaw clenches when his tongue is back on me, sending hot waves of delight surging through my body. He keeps a steady rhythm for a while, long enough to feel an orgasm coming on.

I grab my breasts and squeeze them as he slips

his fingers back in me. "Fuck, you've got me all worked up," he says in a low and gritty voice. It's filled with lust and desire and sends me closer to the edge. "My cock is so hard for you."

"Fuck me with it," I moan. I squeeze my eyes tight and swallow hard. I don't speak like this. I don't say these words. But Dex is driving me crazy. He's turning me into a sex-crazed animal. All I want is his cock in me. "Please." I can hear the desperation in my voice.

"Oh, I will," he says as he slides his fingers in and out. "I'm definitely going to fuck this tight, wet, sexy little pussy, but first, you're going to come on my lips."

He licks me faster and with a hungry desperation to make me come. I'm so focused on his tongue inside of me that I don't notice my orgasm coming on until it's too late.

"Come for me, Riley," he purrs, holding me tight like he's never going to let me go. "Make this tight little pussy come on my lips."

His sexy words send me over the edge, and I come for him. I bite my lip to keep from screaming out as I come on his mouth, just like he demanded.

I can't talk. I can barely swallow. I can hardly breathe as the intense waves of pleasure surge through my body all the way to my core. He keeps his fingers inside of me and grunts as I roll my hips, pressing down against his hungry mouth, which is still pressed up against me, dragging me deeper into bliss.

"That's a good girl," he says as he stands up and kisses me on the mouth. I moan on his tongue, tasting my own tangy juices as my legs tremble so hard that I don't think I could take a step without falling. Luckily, I'm in water so when he releases my mouth I let my body drop and sink to the bottom of the pool.

I close my eyes under the cool refreshing water as I blow out bubbles, enjoying the last of the waves of pleasure within that are only now starting to dissipate.

I've never fooled around in a pool before, but I like it. It feels so nice to cool off my burning skin in the invigorating water after an intense orgasm.

Dex leaves me for a minute, letting me lie on the bottom of the pool until my lungs are burning and I have to come back up for air.

The sight that greets me is a beautiful one: Dex is naked in the water, gripping his long hard dick with his hand, stroking it slowly as he looks at me.

There are so many things I want to do to him. I want him to feel as good as he made me feel.

"Have you ever touched yourself like this while thinking of me?" My voice is so throaty. I barely recognize it.

"Of course," he groans as I close the distance between us. My hand replaces his and starts stroking his thick shaft with long slow strokes. "The first time I saw you in the jet, I was hard for the entire plane ride after. I've never come so hard as when I think of you."

A thrill rushes through me as I picture him touching himself as he thinks of me. I want to peer into his mind and see what he was fantasizing about so I can make it a reality.

"You don't have to imagine it anymore," I say, pressing my palm to his chest. "I'm all yours."

I gently push his chest and he starts walking

backward, letting me guide him. I think he would let me lead him anywhere as long as I'm stroking his cock like this.

"Sit," I command when he arrives at the stairs leading into the pool.

He does as I say and it makes me smile. It's my turn to be in control.

I drop to my knees as he sits on the second stair that's barely submerged in the water. His cock looks intimidatingly big the closer I get to it. It's so big and hard and velvety with droplets of water dripping down his stiff shaft.

My heart thumps wildly in my chest as I open my mouth and take him in. He lets out a long deep groan as I swirl my tongue on the tip of his head, lapping up his pre-cum.

His fingers thread through my wet hair, gripping my head as he guides me up and down on his cock. "Fuck, Riley," he groans as I open wider, picking up the pace.

I give him the royal treatment; massaging, licking, and sucking with my greedy tongue and hungry lips.

I've never really enjoyed giving head before. I always felt like it was something that I should be doing and not something that I wanted to be doing. But here, in the lit-up pool under the dark Caribbean night sky, I'm enjoying having Dex's cock in my mouth. I'm absolutely loving it.

His groans start to come out deeper and lower as I coat his dick with my saliva. His breaths come out in hisses, and he starts whispering my name.

"I'm going to come," he groans, dropping his head back as I bob my head up and down.

I suck him even harder, wanting to taste him, needing him to release into my mouth. And he does.

His cock tightens in my hand and then pulses, coating my mouth with his warm cum. He grunts my name, but I can hardly hear him over my own moaning.

I've never swallowed before, but I greedily drink him down and then suck on his tip for any reluctant drops.

He smiles when he finally raises his head and opens his heavy eyelids.

"That was fun," I say, still stroking his cock and wanting more.

Dex's eyes narrow on me, sending shivers racing through my body. "That was just the beginning," he growls. "Get your things. We're going back to the room."

# CHAPTER SEVENTEEN

## *DEX*

"I'm going to fuck you into a coma."

Riley grins, looking excited for it as I march over to the bed that I just threw her on. We just had a little appetizer in the pool, but now I'm ready for the main course.

And this time, I'm not holding back.

She lets out an audible gulp as I yank off my shirt and toss it behind me, advancing on her like a lion about to attack a wounded gazelle.

A growl escapes my throat as she opens her legs for me. She's got those tight yoga pants back on, the ones that make her ass look perfectly round. Her shirt was long enough to double as a dress but I made her put those hot pants back on just so I could undress her again.

I'm going to enjoy this.

Every second of it.

"Are you going to fuck me now?"

Her voice is deep. Raspy. Teetering on the edge of control.

Riley is already writhing on the bed, staring up at me with the most beautiful eyes that are clouded with lust.

She's perfect.

I've already come in that greedy little mouth of hers, so now I'm able to take my time with her. I've been waiting for it long enough, dreaming of it, fantasizing about it. I want to make it last.

"You want me to fuck you? You want to feel my hard cock sliding into you?"

"Yes," she moans, arching her back on the bed as her mischievous hand slides down to her pussy. It disappears in her pants, and she stares up at me with glazed-over eyes and parted lips as she plays with herself.

"I've wanted you so bad," she moans, looking like she's being tortured as she rubs her pussy. "I've been pretending like I don't, but it's all I can think about."

"You were touching yourself in the shower when I came in, weren't you?"

"Yes," she moans, her back jerking up as she hits her spot. She bites her bottom lip and moans, closing her eyes as her legs start to shake.

My dick is rock hard, but I'm not ready to whip it out just yet. This show is too good.

"Show me," I say, swallowing hard. "Show me how you play with your tight little pussy."

She shakes her head on the pillow, but she's smiling, her hand moving under her pants like she's a DJ scratching a record.

"No," she groans, grinning as she looks at me

with those hungry eyes. "I hate you. You're the enemy."

"The enemy has won, Riley Coyote," I say, gripping her pants and underwear with both hands. "It's time for my spoils of war. It's time to get what I've been fighting for."

She shakes her head on the pillow. "I'll never surrender."

But her body doesn't match her words. She's not only waving the white flag, she's opening the door to the promised land and pulling me inside.

She plants her feet on the bed and arches her ass off the bed so I can slide off her pants.

My cock is aching in my pants. It's throbbing as I watch her run her sticky fingers over her wet pussy. The sight, the smell-it's all waking something carnal and savage within me.

"Take your shirt off." My voice catches in my throat. Even I can hear the need in it. "I want to see those gorgeous tits of yours."

"Never," she gasps as her free hand reaches up and massages her breast. "I don't show my enemies anything."

"If you want my cock you will."

"I don't negotiate with terrorists." But there's no negotiating. She fists a ball of her shirt and yanks it up her torso, showing off her smooth stomach.

Heat is running through me from my head to my toes. I yank off my shirt as she pulls hers off, quickly undoing her bra as well before dropping back down on the bed.

Her hand darts right back between her legs, and she grins as she looks at me, rubbing her clit in tight little circles.

I lick my lips as I drag my eyes over her perky breasts, her nipples as firm as pebbles. She has a beautiful chest. The nicest I've ever seen, and I've seen a lot.

"If this is how you act in front of your enemies," I say, swallowing as I watch her slip a finger deep in her wet hole. "Then consider me your arch nemesis."

"I already do," she moans. She slips a second finger inside and a throaty moan falls from her lips.

This view is pure fucking heaven, but I have to join in. Her body shivers as I slide my palm up the inside of her leg. She opens her mouth wide and gasps when my hand joins hers, sliding over her wet folds.

My dick jumps as I slide two fingers inside her, feeling her sticky warmth.

"Look how wet you are," I say, sliding out my two fingers and separating them. A sticky snail trail connects my index and middle finger like a silky strand of spider web. "Do you always get this wet when you're around me?"

"Never," she lies with an adorable little grin on her tormented face. "I'm as dry as the Sahara Desert around you."

"Please," I say, raising my juice covered fingers to my lips. "You're as wet as that ocean in the middle of a rain storm."

Her eyes widen as I slip my two fingers in my mouth and suck off her sweet juices. It tastes like sex. It tastes like heaven.

I'm loving the soft noises that she makes, but it's time for me to take over. She whimpers as I grab her wrist with a firm grip and pull her hand away from her spread pussy.

She's breathing so hard, practically panting, as she watches me stand up off the bed and unbuckle my belt. I slowly bring down my zipper, loving that raw desperate look in her eye. Her hand creeps back between her legs as I pull my jeans down, letting my cock spring free.

"Don't touch," I snap. "That's my pussy from now on. You want to touch it, you have to ask me."

Her hand flies back to her breasts, squeezing and massaging them as she watches me with glossy eyes.

"I hate you so much," she moans, licking her sweet lips as she arches her head up to look at my hard cock. "You're the worst."

"And you're an uptight little goodie-goodie who always has to play by the rules." I grip my cock and climb back on the bed. "*My* room. *My* rules."

"It's *our* room," she moans, spreading her legs wider as I climb between them. "And you're a reckless brute who has no manners."

I drag the tip of my cock up her glistening folds, and she cries out, arching her back as she squeezes her nipples. "You don't need manners when you have a dick this big."

She holds her breath as I tease her, tracing the head of my cock around her opening. "Tell me you love me."

"Fuck you."

I laugh. "That's the Riley I wanted. You're so sexy when you're all riled up like this."

I've been playing games with her since the first moment I saw her, saying dirty comments, and making her uncomfortable, trying to get to this moment. I've been jacking up the sexual tension between us, getting her frustrated so she can finally unleash that frustration on my cock.

It's worked like a charm. And now it's time to cash in on all my hard work.

"I'm not riled up," she gasps, shivering as I press my thick shaft against her clit. "I'm perfectly fucking calm."

Her trembling legs are telling a different story.

"Good to know."

I step off the bed and chuckle as her eyes fly open in a panic. Her eyes never leave my cock as I walk up to the head of the bed and climb back on.

She gets to her knees, her hand knuckle deep in her pussy as she watches me sit down. The wooden headboard is freezing against my back but there's so much heat swirling inside my body that I don't care.

"Come here," I say, reaching for her.

She moves into my arms, straddling my legs as she bites her bottom lip. She's glaring at me the entire time.

Her pussy is spread out in front of me as she lowers her hips, bringing her hot sex down on my hard shaft. It feels so fucking soft and wet. I just want to grab my dick and slide inside her, but that's what a lover would do.

We're enemies after all.

She grips the headboard behind me with both hands as she starts rocking her hips on me, making my heart pound in my chest.

"You hate me?"

"Yes." She gasps out the word as she grinds her clit against my throbbing dick. "I hate the shit out of you."

"Good," I say, grabbing her waist with two strong hands. "Fuck me like you hate me."

She reaches down, grabbing my dick with an eager hand. We both throw our heads back and moan as she guides my dick into her wet hole.

"God, Riley," I whisper as she lowers her hips, engulfing me with her hot tightness. She's so wet, and I slide in easily despite the snug fit.

There's no easing into it. There's no taking it slow.

She drops all the way down, taking all of me in with one desperate rush of her hips.

Her hard nipple drags over my lips as she moves up and down and I pounce on her tits, grabbing them, massaging them, licking, and sucking her nipples until she's moaning my name.

She's gripping the headboard behind me so hard that it sounds like it's going to snap as she slams up and down on my cock, her tight pussy squeezing me with a death grip.

I knew she was *uptight*, but I know she was so *damn tight*.

She picks up the pace, pumping up and down in a frenzy. I move my hands around to her flawless ass and dig my fingertips into her cheeks, spreading them apart as she fucks me.

"Tell me you love me."

She looks down at me with nothing but lust and frustration on her face.

"Never," she moans, dropping her head back. Her silky brown hair is violently bouncing on her shoulders, making my dick even harder. "You're the enemy."

That's not good enough.

"Say it."

She whimpers as I give her ass a hard squeeze, but she doesn't miss a beat, driving those ferocious hips up and down on my cock.

Her breaths are raging, her chest rising and falling viciously. Her eyes are half closed as she clenches her jaw, moaning with every frustrated movement.

I grab the back of her neck and pull her down, her lips a heartbeat away from mine and whisper. "Say it."

Her mouth shoots open as her swollen clit slams onto my pelvis, her warm breath washing over my hungry lips. "Say it."

She opens her mouth as she leans over me, her soft hair tickling my face. Our lips are so close. I can hear her heart pounding.

"Fuck you," she whispers onto my mouth. I smile as she crushes her lips to mine, plunging her tongue into my mouth as I wrap my arms around her, holding her as tight as I can without breaking her.

I push her down on the bed, never leaving her hot tightness as I fall with her into the missionary position. "You're going to pay for that," I warn.

Her eyes sparkle as she looks at me with a challenging look on her face. "I hope so."

I fuck her hard and fast, burying myself to the hilt with every powerful thrust. She wraps her legs around me, hooking her ankles like she never wants to let me go. That's just fine with me. I'm in heaven right here, and I would be happy to spend an eternity doing this with my angel.

"You've lost the war," I groan into her ear. "This is what happens when you lose to me. Wifey."

"It's all part of my plan," she moans, writhing under me. She grabs a fistful of sheets and yanks it off the mattress. "You'll see."

The sight of her naked under me, her voluptuous body shining with a sexy coat of sweat is so erotic that I have to look away before I end the night too early.

Her face is perfect, all twisted up in pained arousal. Her luscious lips tempt me with every stunning movement. I groan when I see her soft pink tongue, and I just have to kiss her.

I'm trying to be gentle, but there's so much intense emotion and need boiling inside of me that I can't.

I bring my lips down on hers in a rough, hard kiss, claiming her mouth and taking what's mine. She kisses me back with equal urgency, making my head spin. When I release her, her teeth grab a hold of my bottom lip, tugging on it as we separate.

This is more perfect than I thought it would be. Our bodies are melting together like they were made for each other.

It's better than any dirty fantasy that I've ever come up with.

I move inside of her fast and hard. She tilts her hips up for more, clawing at my back as she cries out. She's close to coming. I can tell. Every cry leaving her mouth is louder, more primal, more desperate.

I really let her have it, the headboard slamming into the wall with each savage thrust.

"Fuck!" she screams as she grips me tight, clinging onto me like I'm the only thing keeping her from spiraling into the abyss. The orgasm rips through her, shaking her to the core.

Her warm juices coat my cock as she comes on me, her tight little pussy squeezing me as hard as she is.

She's breathing so heavy as I slowly drag my cock out inch by heavenly inch, feeling her tight grip around my shaft.

"Still hate me?" I ask when her breath calms, the most intense part of her orgasm finally over.

"No," she says with a laugh. "I'll marry you for real."

I smile as I slide my cock back in her, giving her slow, easy thrusts until she's ready to go again.

"I might take you up on that."

"Will your cock be my maid of honor?" she asks, smiling as she runs her hand through her hair. "Because it's my new best friend."

The moment is so perfect and I never want it to end. I wish I could lock the door and keep her here with me forever.

We kiss softly, enjoying the slow pace until our bodies start demanding more. My rhythm speeds up, giving her longer, deeper, harder strokes.

I take her earlobe in my mouth and nibble on it. "You said you can do the splits?"

"Oh, God."

"Show me."

She puts two hands on my chest and gently pushes me off of her. We both moan when my dick slides out of her.

I stroke myself as I watch her climb off the bed and stand in front of me. She's so beautiful. I want to see her naked in every position. From every angle.

Her brown hair is a wild mess hanging down over the top of her breasts, but it looks gorgeous. Her nipples are calling out to me, teasing me as the shimmering buds beg me to wrap my lips around them.

"I'm only going to do this once," she says, her cheeks flushing as she grabs her ankle. She raises her foot over her head in a full splits. Her legs are a perfectly straight line with her glistening pussy smack in the middle.

I'm off the bed in an instant, grabbing her raised ankle and holding it there. She holds onto the dresser for support as I grab my throbbing cock and slide it back inside of her where it belongs.

"Just like I pictured," I groan, as I thrust in and out.

Her eyes are squeezed shut as she holds her breath. "It's so fucking deep," she moans as I saw her back and forth.

I pull back a little for her, but she grabs my ass in a panic. "No," she gasps, pulling me back into her.

She moans as I fill her with swift thrusts, enjoying every second of it.

We catch each other's eye in the mirror across the room and seeing her face all twisted up in agony sends me spiraling. Her brow is furrowed, her mouth wide open in an O shape, her gorgeous tits swinging back and forth with every powerful thrust.

My mouth becomes dry with anticipation as I feel an orgasm raging forward, clawing through me in an unstoppable wave.

Our eyes are locked on each other's through the mirror as we both come at the same time.

It hits me like a truck, and I hold onto her for support as I pump one final time inside her. She crumples onto the dresser, dropping her leg as her orgasm consumes her. I step on my toes, pushing deep inside her as I empty every last drop of my seed into her tight little pussy.

We never break eye contact through the whole experience, even when I feel her pulse around me, pulling out every drop that I have for her.

It becomes too much and our legs give out. We drop to the floor in a hot sweaty mess of cramping limbs and exhausted groans.

Riley curls up onto me. She looks so small and delicate in my arms.

I reach up and grab the sheets from the bed, pulling them down onto the floor. I'd pick her up and carry her onto the mattress, but my legs and arms feel like lead, and I can't hold myself up at the moment, let alone her too.

"Mmmm," she moans as I wrap the blankets around her. I drop my head against the dresser as I turn to look at our reflection in the mirror.

We look so perfect like this, in each other's arms on the floor. I hope she realizes it now. I hope she sees.

"Is the war over?" I whisper, kissing the top of her head. The smell of her fruity shampoo is making me dizzy.

"No," she whispers back but there's a smile on her calm face. She looks so peaceful wrapped up in the blankets with her eyes closed. "This is all part of my genius plan."

"Look over there, Napoleon," I say, gently guiding her chin toward the mirror. She smiles as she sees our reflection. "Does that look like two people at war?"

She slowly shakes her head. "That looks like two different puzzle pieces that somehow fit."

We sit like this for a while until her body starts shaking with giggles.

"What?"

"I knew it."

"Knew what?"

She covers her mouth with the blanket as she lets out an adorable giggle. "You only came when you saw yourself in the mirror. I knew it all along. You *are* in love with yourself."

I make her pay by squeezing my arms around her. "Well, someone has to love me. Especially when the girl I'm falling for keeps calling me her enemy."

She smiles as she rests her head on my bicep, watching me through the mirror. "You're not so bad."

I hold her like this for hours, ignoring my legs that are exploding with pins and needles and fighting my eyelids that keep trying to close.

Riley fell asleep hours ago, but I want to stay up as long as I can. I don't want this beautiful moment to ever end.

Because when we wake up in the morning we'll be enemies again.

And I don't know if I'll ever get another chance at this sliver of heaven.

# CHAPTER EIGHTEEN

*RILEY*

"Mmmm," I moan, feeling like I'm waking up after being in a coma for over a decade. My whole body feels sluggish and sore, like there's liquid metal running through my veins.

*So, this is what it feels like to wake up after being gorilla fucked by a hot pilot. Totally worth it.*

I turn my head on the soft pillow looking for Dex, but his side of the bed is empty. The bathroom door is open and the light is off as well. I don't see him anywhere.

My first reaction is not a good one.

I immediately think that he left. That he was using me all along and that he just struck the final deathblow in our little war.

My body tenses as I sit up in the bed trying to turn my sadness into anger when I see a note on the table with a tropical flower lying beside it.

I'm out of the bed in a flash and scurrying across the cold tiles in my bare feet. I pick up the flower and the note, slip on one of Dex's t-shirts, and walk out back where it's cloudy but nice and warm. Our room is on the ground level with a view of the north side of the island where the waves are violent and vicious, yet beautiful and humbling at the same time.

The waves are bigger than normal today, and the sheer size and power of them takes my breath away as they relentlessly crash onto the rocky shore.

I sit in the chair and smell the flower before reading the note. Dex's handwriting is scribbled across the paper, and I smile at the little hearts that he used to dot the I's.

*Good morning beautiful,*

*The waves were looking almost as spectacular as you.*
*I couldn't resist.*
*Enjoy the show…*

*- Dex*

*P.S. There's fresh coffee in the pot. ;)*

I lower the note (and my jaw) when I look up and see Dex surfing on the waves. My initial shock turns to worry, which quickly turns to awe when I see how skilled he is on the board. He cuts through the waves like a shark, turning the surfboard with complete control. He moves with such grace and ease, gliding across the monstrous wave like a superhero.

I run inside and quickly grab a coffee as he surfs out of a wave and lowers his belly onto the board. I don't want to miss a thing, so I hurry back with my steaming cup and watch as he paddles back behind the break of the waves.

He puts on quite the show as he picks the largest waves to surf down. His movements are so smooth, so beautiful. He's human. Water isn't our element. He shouldn't be so graceful and controlled, so skilled and poised, yet somehow he is.

*Maybe he is a shark after all.*

I smell the flower and smile as I watch him fall off his board and crash into the water with his feet over his head. He's not a shark. He's a puffer fish. All tough talk and attitude, but he's really sweet inside.

He looks right at me when he pops out of the water. He has a big smile on his face as he waves to me before grabbing onto his board.

I sit up straight in my chair and try to smooth out my hair the best that I can as he paddles toward the shore like a sexy turtle.

Last night was incredible. Pure magic. I've always enjoyed sex, but I've never been obsessed with it. I never understood why people could throw everything away, families, careers, their lives, for an hour of fun. Now I know. Now I get it.

Dex opened my eyes in a big way.

I hadn't planned on it. Actually, I had planned against it.

But every once in a while, a woman just has to let herself have some fun.

I take a sip of my coffee and laugh to myself. *Like you ever had a chance.* He was in complete control of my body from the first touch. I would have done anything with him. Anything *for* him.

I would have married him and had all his babies if he only would have asked.

I would have jumped off a cliff if he would have suggested it. I would have stuck a knife in my heart for his amusement.

I was his *slave*.

And I loved every second of it.

Nervous butterflies flutter in my stomach as he gets out of the water and smiles at me. I don't know how today is going to go.

What does he want?

What do I want?

I have no idea. *Maybe another round in the bedroom to help me think…*

We got along great last night, but that was because our clothes were off. It's easy not to say things that will piss the other person off when your jaw is shut tight and the only noises you're making are groans and moans. Our relationship usually gets into trouble when Dex opens his mouth.

I'm really hoping it's going to be different now. It would just be cruel to have sex that good with someone and then never have it again.

I'm getting wet just thinking about it. I haven't even finished my coffee, and I'm already craving a big cock in my mouth.

*Oh, my God. Am I whore?*

If I am, it's Dex's fault. He's a master at the art of making love. He's skilled with every part of his body: his hands, his lips, his cock, his fingers, his tongue… Oh God, his tongue. It's what miracles are made of.

I had never come during sex before last night. The few sexual partners I did have never got me going the way that he did. It was incredible, like I had left my body and ascended to another plane of existence-one where multiple orgasms were as easy to get as parking tickets.

Three of them. All stronger and harder than the last.

"Good morning," he says as he arrives with the surfboard tucked under his arm.

He leans in and gives me a soft kiss on the lips as if it's the most natural thing in the world. Desire starts flowing through me as he stands back up. Droplets of water fall from his wet messy hair onto my shirt as I lick my lips, tasting the saltiness from the ocean.

"Good morning," I answer with a whimper. *It's a good morning now.*

I gulp as I admire his hard body that's still soaking wet. He's wearing the colorful boardshorts that I like, the ones that rest a little too low on his hips. They show off the beautifully carved V in his pelvis and just a hint of his dark pubic hair.

He rests the surfboard against the villa as I groan, watching his back muscles ripple with every movement. He's so beautiful. The perfect view to wake up to.

"I didn't know you surf," I say, catching a glimpse of his shredded abs as he turns around. I haven't moved from my chair, but my heart is beating like I just ran a marathon.

He sits in the chair beside me and smiles. "There's a lot that you don't know about me."

"I think I already know too much," I say, chuckling as I take a sip of my coffee.

Dex reaches over and slides his hand on mine,

taking the coffee mug from my hand. "That's not what you were saying last night," he says with a grin. He takes a sip of my coffee, turning the mug to place his lips on the exact place where I drank from and then hands it back. "You were crying out for more."

"I was not," I answer playfully. "I think you might need your hearing checked."

"I think you're right," he says with a grin. "You were screaming into my ear so loud that I think I burst an eardrum."

Typical cocky Dex. I hate that his arrogant attitude is actually doing something for me now. Maybe it's because he deserves to be arrogant and cocky after his performance last night.

"But seriously," I say, trying to change the subject. "Where did you learn to surf like that?"

"Hawaii," he says, resting his hands on his abs. His beautiful, hard, mouthwatering abs. "Marv vacations there from time to time. We were there for three weeks last May, and I spent the entire time surfing."

"Wow," I say, looking out at the thrashing waves in the ocean. "That sounds fun."

"It will be more fun with you there. Although I'm not sure if we'll be doing much surfing."

"What will we be doing?" I ask, raising a questioning eyebrow at him.

He glances over his shoulder at the king-sized bed that's calling our name. "Come inside and I'll show you."

I'm tempted, even though I'm still sore from last night. "Let me finish my coffee first."

He looks disappointed until I down it in one gulp. I toss the mug onto the sand and stand up. "I'm ready."

After a quick romp and a shower, Dex and I head down for breakfast. I'm so hungry that I could eat a horse, raw.

I can't help but wonder what it's going to be like when we no longer have to pretend that we're husband and wife. Are we going to go back to our old fighting like cats and dogs ways, or is it going to be different?

Dex slides his hand over mine, and I instantly feel better. The hallway is empty and we don't have to pretend anything, but he still holds my hand.

"So," I say, turning away so he doesn't see my cheeks getting red. "Are we like dating now?"

"We're married," he says, looking at me sideways. "Are you divorcing me already?"

It was a serious question, but he answered it with a joke. *I guess I have my answer.*

I shouldn't care. Who in their right mind would want to date Dex? Seriously, I'm better without him. I shouldn't care.

But I do.

I swallow down the sigh that's creeping up my throat and force a smile onto my face. No one likes a clingy girl who doesn't know her place after a one night stand.

"Riley Coyote," Dex says, stopping and dropping to a knee.

I raise an eyebrow as I look down at him.

He takes my hand and looks up at me with the bluest eyes. "Would you be my girlfriend?"

I pull my hand away and cross my arms over my chest, looking down at him skeptically. "Is this some kind of a trick?"

"Yes," he says with a nod. "I'm going to make you fall in love with me, marry me, have my children, grow old by my side, and then, when you least expect it, I'll strike."

"You'll strike?"

"I'll strike."

I chuckle as I look at him, still kneeling on the ground. He's clearly joking, but a small part of me still isn't sure.

"No."

He drops his head and lets out a frustrated sigh. "Why not?"

"We're enemies. I don't date my enemies. It's War 101. Never date your enemy. That's why President Roosevelt and Hitler never hooked up. I'm surprised you didn't know that."

He rolls his eyes as he looks up at me. "Did you just compare me to Hitler?"

I shrug my shoulders. "Well, come on. If one of us has to be Hitler in this scenario, it's not going to be me."

Dex glances down at his knee that's still on the floor. "Are you going to say yes or should I get up?"

"I'm really hungry."

"Okay then," he says, shaking his head as he gets to his feet. He looks upset. Genuinely upset.

It makes me feel better.

"All right," I say, stepping in close to him. I

206

take a deep breath and hold it as I press my finger to his soft lips and hold it there. "I'll be your girlfriend."

His eyes light up, but he doesn't say a word, mainly because I have my index finger pressed against his mouth.

"Don't get too excited," I say, narrowing my eyes as I stare up at him. "It's only because I like to keep my friends close but my enemies closer."

I remove my finger, expecting a witty comeback, but he gives me a soft romantic kiss instead. My head is spinning when he pulls away and takes my hand.

"Come," he says, pulling me down the hallway. "My girlfriend is hungry. Let's get her fed."

I'm smiling so much that my cheeks are burning as we rush down the hallway toward the dining room. We stop before the door when we hear Marv's and Prince Kalib's voices inside.

Dex looks at me, and I can tell he's thinking the same thing that I am. We don't want to go in there and let these people ruin this nice moment.

"Come," he whispers, pulling me in the opposite direction. He opens a service door and pulls me into the kitchen. There are three chefs inside. The closest one to us is leaning against the wall, smoking a cigarette. He throws it into a jar of mayonnaise in a panic when he sees us barge in.

"Good morning," the chef says, a cloud of smoke floating out of his mouth as he speaks. The other two chefs straighten up as they see us, thrusting their shoulders back like we're some kind of royalty.

"We need food to go," Dex says, looking around as he rushes forward.

I walk up to the slacker chef as Dex gets busy

grabbing muffins and fruit from the stainless steel tables. The chef cringes as I look into the jar of mayo with the cigarette butt stuck in it.

"Can you make Kara's sandwich with that?" I ask.

He looks confused. I don't think he speaks English.

"Let's go," Dex says, waving me over.

"Au revoir," I say to the chefs as we disappear through the back door. We're outside, and the sun is finally starting to creep through the clouds.

"What do you want to do?" he asks, handing me a blueberry muffin that he grabbed. "We can do anything you want."

"Anything?"

"Anything!"

There are two things I want to do, and one is ruled out because my pussy is sore and needs a break.

"Would you take me flying?"

He rubs his chin as he thinks about it. "Under one condition."

"What?"

"You're in the driver's seat."

"Careful," Dex warns as he fidgets in his seat. "Your right wing is dipping."

My pulse is racing as fast as the engine as I come in for the landing. I adjust the yoke, bringing the wing up and trying to stay level as we float down to the ocean.

I did everything.

The checks, the take-off, the navigation, the flying, and now I'm landing the plane.

Dex watches my every movement, every flick of my wrist as I guide the plane down. He nods in approval as I hit the switch to open the flaps.

"Good," he says as the flaps grind on their way down. The plane jerks back and my heart skips a beat. "It's okay," he says, placing a comforting hand on my leg. "That's just the flaps slowing us down. You're doing great."

Adrenaline is coursing through my body as I check the instrument panel. I've had a wide grin on my face since I stepped onto the plane, and it's not going away anytime soon.

I'm flying a plane without a license. This is so not like me.

But I'm loving it. I'm having the time of my life.

Dex has taught me that a little recklessness can be a good thing once in a while. *Easy, Riley. Land the plane first.*

It may not be a good idea after all if I land the plane in a fiery ball of crushed metal and flames. But I have everything under control. I've flown the flight simulator on my computer enough that I'm feeling pretty comfortable. And there's a hot, skilled pilot sitting on my right who can take over if things get too much for me.

"Nice and easy," he says as we float down to the ocean where I'm going to be landing. "Your runway is huge. If you miss it, then I'm afraid you're not going to make it as a pilot."

I laugh as I hit the switch to lower the flaps

again. The plane slows to a crawl. I wipe my sweaty palms on my shorts and grab the yoke, squeezing it tightly as I aim for the calm water.

Dex leans over, just in case, and even his musky scent can't distract me for long.

"Power back," he says. "Gently."

I do as he says, getting nervous as the water gets closer.

We're so close that I can see little tropical fish under the water scatter as we are about to touch down.

"Power back all the way," he says through my headset. "Pull back the yoke. All the way. Pull! Pull! Pull!"

I yank the yoke back all the way until my arms are shaking. I take a deep breath and hold it as the pontoons slam into the water, jerking us up against our seatbelts.

The nose of the plane drops down and I release my breath, staring through the windshield as the plane bobs up and down on the water.

"Yes!" Dex yells, pumping his fist.

I'm sitting as still as a statue, staring at the slow-moving propeller. "You might want to take your headset off," I calmly warn him.

He quickly yanks it off his head, and I let out a scream so loud that my throat burns. "Woo!" I shout, hooting and squealing as I slap the roof over my head.

"That's what I'm fucking talking about!" Dex shouts, joining in my celebration. He gives me a hard high-five and holds my hand, squeezing it as he smiles at me. "You did it!"

I slip off my headset and smooth out my hair,

taking deep breaths to try and calm the adrenaline ripping through me.

It was incredible. I flew a freaking plane!

"You're not done yet, Captain," Dex says, pointing at the open ocean in front of us. The plane was drifting away during my little freakout. "Let's beach this baby and celebrate!"

I taxi the plane to the beach, driving it onto the sand. I cut the engine and take out the key, staring at it in my hand.

"How do you feel?"

"Lucky," I say. The word catches in my throat.

"You are lucky," he says, rubbing his chin. "Not many people ever get to fly a plane."

But I don't feel lucky because of the flying. I feel lucky because I met Dex.

"Yeah," I say, swallowing hard as I open my hand. I give him the key and meet his eyes.

I feel so emotional. Tears well up in my eyes as my chin trembles. "Thank you," I whisper.

"No problem," he says, giving me a wink. He's acting like it's nothing. He's acting like he didn't just make a lifelong dream come true. He's acting like I'm not falling in love with him at this exact moment.

"Just a regular day as my girlfriend."

"Really," I say, laughing as I wipe my eyes with the back of my hand. "I can't wait to see what you have planned for tomorrow."

"We're going to the moon."

We both laugh.

He reaches forward, cups my cheek, and wipes the wetness from my eye with his thumb. "Come," he says, smiling the sexiest smile that I've ever seen. "I'll buy you a beer. Pilot."

The gesture is so simple, wiping away my tear, but it means the world to me. It's then that I drop the whole enemy thing. There's no more war.

I'm ready to surrender myself to him and let the chips fall where they may.

I'm ready to be a little wild and reckless. I'm ready to go to the dark side.

We get out and secure the plane, and before I get that beer that he promised me, a butler comes running up the beach.

"Mr. Dex," he says, bowing his head. "Mr. Gladstone would like to have a word with you as soon as possible."

"Shit," Dex curses under his breath. "Tell him I'm busy."

"I'm afraid this can't wait," he says with a tight expression on his face. "He said it was an emergency."

Dex looks at me and I shake my head. "Go," I say. "We have all the time in the world after."

He sighs and then turns back to the butler. "This better be good," Dex says. "You're making me stand up my girlfriend."

The sound of that word on his lips gives me goosebumps.

"Where is he?"

"He's waiting in the helicopter on the roof," the butler says, waving him toward the sprawling villa. "I'll show you."

Dex tilts his head as he watches the man. "I'm not trained to fly that thing."

"Let's just go check it out," I say, feeling like something is wrong.

The butler holds up his hand and cringes at me. "I'm afraid that he requested that Dex comes alone."

"What?" Dex shouts, stepping forward as he looks up at the roof.

I grab his tattooed arm and tug it back. "I'll be fine," I say as butterflies invade my stomach. "Just go see what he wants."

He gives me a quick kiss and then leaves me on the beach with my lips tingling and my stomach in knots.

# CHAPTER NINETEEN

## *DEX*

*I'm getting sick of billionaires.*

This better be good.

"You better be dying up here," I say as I burst through the door onto the roof. The Augusta helicopter is sitting on the helipad like a sleeping monster. "You're cockblocking me big time, Marv."

I shield my eyes from the sun as I walk over with the butler following me close behind. His head is practically on my shoulder.

"*Fuck*," I curse under my breath when I arrive at the helicopter and see who's inside.

It ain't Marv.

It's Kara. She's sprawled across the Captain's chair wearing only a pilot's hat. She has the helicopter's instruction manual resting on her lap hiding her pussy, but her tits are in full glorious view.

The butler seems to like them. He's panting as he looks over my shoulder.

I look back at him and raise an eyebrow. "Mr. Gladstone wanted me? Really dude?"

He just shrugs. "She showed me her boobs."

Fucking men.

"Well, you two have fun," I say, walking back to the door.

"Wait, Dexy," Kara calls out. I stop with a sigh. She's going to keep doing this, but maybe next time it will be worse. Maybe next time Riley will be with me.

The butler is watching, looking like he stuffed a banana from the breakfast buffet into his pants.

"You can leave us," I say, slapping a hand on his shoulder.

His face drops as he lets out a disappointed sigh. "I can stay," he says, never taking his eyes off of Kara's perky tits. "In case you need anything."

I grab the back of his shirt and nearly lift him off his feet. "I need you to get the hell out of here and make sure that Mrs. Riley doesn't come up."

The butler grins at me. "Don't worry," he says. "I'll make sure you're not interrupted. If you do one thing for me."

"What?"

"Slap that ass for me once."

He'd better leave before I toss him off the roof. "It's not like that."

He just laughs as he takes one last look at Kara and then backs away toward the door. "Yeah right. No man can turn *that* down."

I gulp as he walks through the door and closes it. I hope he's wrong.

"Dexy," Kara moans, arching her back as she looks at me with lush pouty lips. The pilot's hat is tilted on her head with her thick blonde curls pouring out. She squeezes her arms together, pressing her tits and perfectly round pink nipples up. I look away, staring up at the rotary blades on top of the helicopter instead.

*Don't look down. Don't look down.*

"I've been trying to get my engine going," she says in a little girl voice as she strokes the instruction manual on her lap, "but I can't. I need your *skilled* hands to help get me going."

I don't take the bait. I just stare up at the blades with my hands on my hips. "Why are you naked?"

"I'm not," she says, turning in the seat to face me. I can see out of the corner of my eye as she places her right leg on the dashboard, spreading her legs for me. "The instruction manual is covering most of it."

She drops it on the ground and it lands with a smack. "Oops."

I swallow hard as it takes everything I have not to look down at her spread pussy.

I've been dreaming of this moment for years. Not only have I been fantasizing about it, I've been scheming and plotting, trying to make it a reality.

And now that it's happening, I'd rather be anywhere but here.

I'm not about to let Kara get in the way of what I have with Riley. Nothing is worth ruining that, especially not her.

"Come help me out, *Mr. Pilot*," she says. The sex and lust are clear in her voice. "I need your *high thrust* capabilities."

She starts moaning as she rubs herself, and

216

suddenly it feels incredibly hot up here.

"Come hit my landing strip," she says, her busy hand working between her legs.

I still haven't looked. But even the strongest men can turn weak at the sticky hands of a masturbating Hidden Pleasures model.

"Why are you doing this?" I ask, breathing heavy despite my not looking. My heart is pounding so hard. "Is it because I'm with Riley now?"

"Who, her?" she asks, the hardness back in her voice. "Don't bring that trash up. You're going to make me lose my lady boner."

"She's not trash," I say, feeling heat flush through me, only now it's not arousal, it's anger. "She's my girlfriend."

"Your *fake* girlfriend."

"Not anymore. I'm in love with her."

Kara steps out of the helicopter and struts forward, swaying her round hips as she comes.

I stare at a small piece of rust on the rotary blade as I hold my breath.

"You're in love with her?" she asks, standing in front of me. She reaches out and drags her hand across my chest. "I can help cure you of that."

She starts unbuttoning my shirt, and I grab her wrist, my heated eyes falling down on hers. "That's enough."

Kara takes a step back. The sexy act is gone. She glares at me like a cornered cat. "*You're* turning *me* down? For *her*?"

"Definitely," I say, my voice firm and unmoving. "She's the one for me."

She huffs out a breath as she looks me up and down with her hand on her hip. "I'm *Kara Gladstone*," she says, her voice full of disbelief.

"And I'm not interested."

"You're going to pay for this," she says, sticking her finger in my face. "Nobody turns *me* down!"

"All right," I say with a nod. "Are we done here?"

"For now," she says, glaring at me.

She storms off, stomping back to the helicopter, and I turn around and head back to the door with a smile on my face.

Her power over me is gone.

I couldn't care less about her. What I have with Riley is a million times more special than any random sex act, even with a hot Hidden Pleasures model.

We have an intense connection that I still can't seem to fully understand, but I'm loving it so far. Against all odds, we were thrown together, and who am I to deny the will of the universe?

Riley and me together?

It's fate.

It's destiny.

It's inevitable.

And it's the best thing to ever happen to me.

"Get the fucking plane ready!" Marv says, grabbing my arm. I jerk my head back in surprise as he pushes me forward.

He looks pissed, like someone took a swim in

his Scrooge McDuck money pool without asking him.

"What's going on?"

Marv grabs a fistful of his hair and nearly rips it out of his head. He should watch it. He doesn't have much to spare, and all the money in the world won't grow hair back.

"This guy is jerking me around," he says with his nostrils flaring. "I'm done putting up with his shit."

We're outside of the villa, and I can see Riley by the plane in the distance, reading her notes. I can't let Marv leave before he sells the yachts. Riley will be devastated if she finds out that she's not getting her commission.

"Look at this place," I say, waving my hand around. The top of the helicopter is visible on the roof and I gulp, wondering if Kara has gotten her clothes back on yet. "He's rich as shit. He's going to buy them. Making us wait is just a cultural thing."

"It's a cheapskate thing," Marv says, fuming. "I've done business all over the world, and I've never seen shit like this before. Four days we've been here, and I can't get him to talk business."

"I can," I say, placing a hand on his shoulder to try and calm him down. "Riley and I aren't fighting anymore. Let us work together and sell it for you. The prince loves Riley. Give her a chance to earn her commission."

"She's had four days!" Marv says, kicking up sand. "And still, nothing!"

"Give us until the end of the day," I say, locking eyes on him. "If he doesn't buy tonight, we'll be wheels up first thing in the morning."

Marv grinds his teeth as he thinks about it.

"Fine," he barks. "This is your last chance."

Riley catches my eye. She's walking over, looking worried.

*Shit.*

She still thinks that Marv had called me up for an emergency, when in reality it was a naked model who tried to seduce me. Things are going to get mighty awkward if she comes over and asks what's wrong.

"I'll make it happen," I say, trying to quickly end the conversation before Riley arrives. "Have I ever let you down?"

"Yes," he answers. "Every day."

"I won't this time," I say, patting his shoulder before running off to intercept my girl.

"Multiple times on most days," he calls out.

I just ignore him. If I've ever let him down in the past, it was probably because I didn't care about his spoiled billionaire problems.

But I care about this one.

I want to make the sale so Riley's dream of being a pilot can come true.

I'm her boyfriend now, and it's my job to make sure all of her dreams become a reality. I'm not about to drop the ball on my first challenge.

"What's going on?" Riley asks when I arrive. She looks as beautiful as ever. I love how her adorable nose crinkles up when she gets concerned.

"Billionaire stuff," I say, rolling my eyes. I slide my hand on her hip and guide her away from the crazy billionaire and his naked wife that I left on the roof.

"He couldn't figure out how to start the helicopter, and he wanted me to help him," I say with a shrug.

Riley looks up at the top of the helicopter parked on the roof and I cringe. "I didn't see it start."

My face is red. My face is never red.

"I lied and told him I couldn't start it," I say, hurrying away from the scene of the crime. "I didn't want him behind the controls of the rotary blades. Knowing him, he'd cut someone's head off."

"Good thinking," she says, turning back to me. "That could have gotten ugly."

I swallow hard, thinking of Kara's failed seduction. "Yup."

*That could have gotten really ugly.*

# CHAPTER TWENTY

## *RILEY*

"Is this how you spoil your girlfriends?" I ask, grinning as Dex closes the door of the supply closet behind him, plunging us into darkness.

"No," he whispers. I can feel his presence but can't see a thing.

I gasp when he shoves his hand up my skirt and cups my sex. "This is how I spoil my girl*friend*. Girlfriend singular, not plural."

Singular, plural, who gives a fuck when his hand is on me like this?

I drop my head back and moan as he teases my opening with his fingertip. I'm already so wet for him.

I was wet for him while I got changed, when I saw him looking fine in a fitted shirt and tie, when we walked down the hall, and when he pulled me into the janitor's closet and closed the door.

I'm always wet for him.

*I have to start drinking more water.*

His low and gritty voice gives me warm shivers as it comes out like sandpaper in the darkness. "No panties. I love it."

"It's laundry day," I tease, smiling as his fingertip rubs little circles around my wet hole. "It definitely wasn't for you."

I gasp as he slides a finger inside me, slow enough to make my toes curl. I grab his thick forearm and dig my nails into his skin, wanting more.

"Are you sure?" he groans, his beard scratching against my cheek as he kisses my neck. "Because I think you're going commando so I can have access to your hot, tight, dripping wet pussy whenever I want."

A throaty moan falls from my parted lips as he slides in a second finger.

I can't see a thing in the closet, and my lack of sight is only working to amp up my other senses. So, Dex's already incredibly skilled hands feel fucking fantastic sliding in and out of me right now.

I grab a fistful of his shirt and arch up on my toes as he buries his fingers knuckle deep inside me, his palm pressing against my throbbing clit.

I could come like this if I wanted to, but I don't. Dex's cock is way too much fun.

"You like that?" he growls deeply into my ear when I let out a whimper.

"I do." I smile as I bite my bottom lip. "I love the smell of bleach and paint thinner. It makes me so hot."

"Funny girl," he whispers before nibbling on my earlobe. It sends warm shivers cascading down my spine. "Would you prefer that I stop?"

"No," I gasp, holding his hand right where it belongs. "But I would like to role play. You can be the sexy janitor, and I can be the janitor's hot wife."

I can feel him smiling on my neck.

"I want to see you with a mop," I say, gasping as he presses hard on my clit. "That would be so hot," I tease.

"You will see me with a mop after," he says, pushing his body against mine. "This pussy is so fucking wet; your juices will be up to our knees when we're done."

My breath catches when I feel his rock-hard dick press against my thigh.

"Then we should get this over with," I say, reaching for his belt. I grab the smooth leather and pull it out of the buckle. "Let's see what Mr. Janitor is packing."

Dex grabs my wrists and pins me to the wall, holding my hands over my head. My heart is pounding so hard. I can't see a thing, which makes this so much more exhilarating.

He holds my hands up with one hand as he bunches my skirt up with the other. Suddenly his cock slides over my pussy, and I inhale sharply.

His cock feels so good. It's so hard.

My legs are already trembling as he moves his hands to the back of my thighs and easily lifts me in the air, pinning my back to the wall.

I'm so wet. My head is spinning with desire and need as he positions himself between my legs, lifts me up, and then slowly brings me down onto his cock.

It slides in easily.

I grip his shoulders and moan loudly as he

thrusts up inside of me, making me forget where we are, making me forget my own name.

We don't last long.

The slow, soft, take-our-time sex was earlier this afternoon. This is a hard and dirty quickie before dinner. But not too dirty. There is a shelf of cleaning products beside my head after all.

His big flexed arms are as hard as his dick as he holds me up. He's so strong. Every hard muscle is like heaven to touch.

"I'm going to come," he groans into my ear.

My hands run over his soft shirt, feeling his taut back muscles underneath. He picks up the pace even more, driving into me relentlessly.

Our bodies give in at the same time, pulsing in simultaneous orgasms. He roots himself deep within me, and I can feel his huge cock jump and pulse before filling me with his thick, hot cum.

I come hard, digging my mouth into his round shoulder to keep from screaming out as the intense waves of heated pleasure flow through me, from my lowered head to my curled toes.

He lowers me to the ground and we rest against each other as we try to catch our breaths.

"I have bad news," I say. My throat is burning.

"What?"

"I'm leaving you for the janitor."

Dex laughs. "We didn't even make it past twenty-four hours."

"Sorry," I say as I smooth my skirt back down. "The janitor has got a *huge* cock. It's over."

"That's okay," he says as I hear the clinking of his belt buckle. "I kind of have a thing for the janitor's hot wife."

"Watch her," I say, grinning in the darkness. "I hear she eats men alive."

Dex chuckles. "Sounds like her."

"Shut up," I say, playfully smacking his arm.

"Are you presentable?" he asks.

"Despite the cum leaking down my inner thighs, yes."

"Sorry about that," he says, feeling around in the darkness. "I saw some paper towels somewhere around here."

"No," I say, resting a hand on him. I think it's his arm, but he's so hard all over that it's hard to tell. "It feels good like this."

I clench my pussy and moan as I feel his sticky load inside of me. I want to keep it in me throughout dinner. It will be a hot secret just for us.

"Ready?" he asks when I hear him grabbing the door handle.

"For round two?"

"For dinner. Round two is for dessert."

"Mmmm," I moan, licking my lips. "Then let's get dinner over with."

He opens the door and I flinch, turning my eyes away from the painfully bright sunlight. We wait for a second or two for our eyes to get adjusted and sneak out. Dex closes the door and we walk casually down the hall like two completely innocent people who totally didn't just have sex.

"What was going on in there?"

*Oh, no.*

"Shit," Dex curses.

I swallow hard as I turn around and see Kara standing against the wall with a smug look on her stupid face. She skips over with her evil eyes sparkling like the fires of hell. I gulp. Kara is only happy when she's about to do some major destruction.

I hold onto Dex's forearm, bracing for impact.

"Well, if it isn't my favorite *fake* couple," she says, skipping over with her hands behind her back. "What was going on in that closet? It didn't sound like you were faking it, Riley. Has the love affair become real?"

"What are you doing?" Dex asks, dropping his hands to his sides. "I think Marv is waiting for you for dinner."

"He can wait."

She looks me up and down, grinning as her eyes meet mine. "I never would have picked her for your taste of the week, Dex."

"Kara." His deep voice comes out like a warning. His eyes are tight and the vein in his neck is twitching. "Don't."

"What?" Kara asks playfully. "I thought you only went for tens. Maybe a nine once in a while."

She steps toward me and curls her finger into a strand of my hair. "She's what? A six? Maybe a six point five if you're on a dry spell, but you're never on a dry spell are you Dex?"

My stomach drops as her words sink into me, making me want to vomit. Has he really been around that much?

She tilts her head and purses her lips when she sees my face. "Ahh," she says, clasping her hands in front of her and giving me puppy dog eyes. "Did you actually think he liked you? That's so cute."

I know she's only saying this stuff to get

under my skin, but it's working. It's what I was worried about all along-that Dex is only using me for sex.

"Did he tell you what he gets if you two sell the yachts?" Her fake-concerned face turns into a wicked grin as she turns to Dex. "Why don't you tell her Dex?"

He won't even look at me.

His face is turning red as he glares at Kara with flared nostrils.

"Dex?" I ask. My voice comes out like the squeak of a chipmunk. "What do you get?"

He still doesn't look at me. He's sweating despite the cool air conditioning.

"What's the matter, Dex?" Kara asks, loving every moment of this. "Pussy got your tongue?"

She smiles as she turns back to me. "I'll tell you since Dex seems to be unusually quiet. He gets your termination papers."

My stomach hardens as I listen to her. I don't want to believe her, but the color draining from Dex's face tells me everything I need to know.

"That's right," Kara says, relishing every second of this. "If Dex helps Marvin make the sale, then you get fired. That's the deal they made. Isn't that right, Dex?"

I turn to him, staring in disbelief.

He finally looks at me with guilty eyes. "That was before. I shouldn't have done it, but I didn't know you back then. I didn't know I would fall for you." His words come out so fast. I can't tell which are true and which are lies.

Was he only pretending to like me, knowing I would be out of his life in a few days?

Kara is grinning like a crazy person. She's loving every second of this.

"Please, Riley," Dex says, stepping forward with his arms out. "Please believe me."

I want to. I desperately want to, but I'm not sure.

I can't think. My thoughts are spinning as I stare at him in disbelief. I knew he was trouble when I first met him, but I didn't think he would try to slam a sledgehammer through my life and ruin it.

Kara walks up to me and places a fake consoling hand on my arm. "You're probably feeling really stupid and embarrassed right now," she says, nodding her head at me. "But don't worry. You have every reason to feel stupid and embarrassed."

*Fuck this!*

I grab her nipple through her sleek dress and squeeze it as hard as I can, turning it like a stubborn dial on an old radio.

"Ow!" she screams, looking at me in horror as she grabs her injured tit.

"Stay the fuck away from me," I warn, slamming my shoulder into her as I barrel past her.

I stop in front of Dex and take a deep breath before looking up at him. My heart seems to momentarily stop.

"I'm sorry, Riley," he says, taking a deep, pained breath. "You know I would have never let you get fired."

"I don't know anything for sure anymore," I say, fighting back tears as I look into his beautiful blue eyes. *Why does he have to be so good looking?*

I smooth out his tie, exhaling long and slow as I try to steel my nerves.

"It was fun," I say, smiling tightly as I try to stop my chin from trembling. "But I think we both know that it was never going to work."

His shoulders drop as all the air huffs out his lungs. He looks crushed.

*It's an act.*

*It's always been an act.*

"Goodbye, Dex."

"Wait," he says, turning to me with his arms out. He has a desperate look on his face. "Where are you going?"

I stop at the entrance of the dining room and turn back to him. My throat is burning as I fight back tears.

"I'm getting my money. And then I'm getting the hell out of here."

# CHAPTER TWENTY-ONE

## *DEX*

"You fucking bitch." I want to snap Kara's neck for that.

"Love you too!" she says, blowing me a kiss before skipping into the dining room, enjoying the wreckage that she just created.

I feel like breaking something.

I feel like burning this place down.

I feel like throwing up.

"Shit," I curse as I loosen my tie. My chest is so tight, and I can hardly breathe. *Why the fuck did she have to do that?*

Things were going so great. And Kara just had to ruin it.

I drop my head and sigh, feeling guilt seep into every cell of my body. *This is your fault.*

*Maybe Riley is right. Maybe I am too reckless.*

I didn't even stop to think of what it would be like for her to get fired. I was only thinking of myself.

231

I probably deserve this.

Does anyone ever deserve to have their heart crushed and broken?

I take a deep breath and follow the girls into the dining room. Prince Kalib is snapping his fingers at the staff, getting them to bring drinks as everyone sits stone-faced at the table.

Marv is sulking with his elbows on a stack of contracts, Kara is glaring at my girl as she holds her right tit, and Riley is downing a glass of wine like she's on stage at Spring Break in a chugging competition.

"Welcome, Dex," Prince Kalib says, waving me over. "I was waiting for everyone to arrive before I extend your invitations for the rest of the week."

"No!" the four of us all shout in a simultaneous panic. The thought of spending a week with any of these people-with the exception of Riley-is making my stomach feel sicker than it already is.

"That's very nice of you," Riley says to the prince. "But unfortunately, we have to get back home. Work obligations."

"Right," the prince says, lowering his head. He was born with a silver shovel in his mouth, and he probably hasn't had to work a day in his life. That's probably why he's so bored that he wants us to stay.

Marv clears his throat. "I'd love to talk to you about the yachts before we leave," he says, rifling through the papers. "I have the contracts here."

I sneak over to Riley and duck down beside her while the prince is distracted. "Can I talk to you for a second?"

Her body is tense. If she was a lioness her claws would be digging into the armrest of the chair. "As my fake husband, my boyfriend, or the asshole who tried to get me fired?" she asks.

I lean into her ear and whisper. "As the janitor."

She chuckles for a second before scowling again. "I'm already clean. Kara's a dirty whore. Why don't you go try with her?"

"Come on, Riley. Let me explain."

"What's to explain? I was nervous on my first day of work, and you tried to get me fired because I didn't give you a blow job."

"Well, when you put it like that, I sound like a total asshole."

She shrugs. "Exactly. At least now you can see yourself through my eyes."

"And what about the past few days? You can't deny that we have a connection."

"I was faking," she says, holding her chin in the air. "As were you, apparently."

"Fine," I whisper as frustration burns through me. "You want to pretend like it was all fake, then fine." I rise to my feet, straighten my shirt, walk to the other side of the table, and grab a chair.

"Here you go, Mr. Jameson," the butler says, handing me a beer.

"Thanks," I mumble, sitting down directly across from my fake wife.

Riley looks at Prince Kalib and smiles.

I grit my teeth together as I stare her down. My world is crumbling down around me and she's smiling. She's fucking smiling!

"Just sign here," Marv says, desperately trying to shove a contract into the prince's hands.

Prince Kalib isn't having any of it. He just turns to Kara, ignoring Marv's borderline frantic words.

*Uh-oh. The big man is going to lose it.*

*He's not the only one.* I'm feeling myself start to slip as well.

"Hey," I whisper, getting Riley's attention. "I love you."

She just crosses her arms and sticks her chin in the air like she didn't hear me or she doesn't care.

"I said I love you," I repeat, leaning on the table. "Does that mean nothing to you?"

Riley turns to me with a glare. "Not from a lying manwhore, it doesn't."

I squeeze my hand into a fist as I drop back into my seat, feeling my blood boil. *A manwhore? She's calling me a manwhore?*

I'll probably have to hand in my man-card after what I turned down this weekend for her. If turning down a beautiful Hidden Pleasures model who was naked and spread eagle for me wasn't enough, I also turned down sixty of the world's most beautiful women who would be eager to obey my every command.

And she calls me a manwhore.

"Prince Kalib," Marv says, waving the papers around angrily. "Sign the contracts. What are we doing here?"

The prince hisses in a long breath and turns to Marv, looking sheepish. "Unfortunately, Mr. Marvin," he says, cringing. "I will not be buying any yachts from you."

Marv's head sounds like a coconut falling as he drops his forehead onto the hard table.

"Why?" Riley asks, looking panicked as she sits up. "What happened to upstaging your brother,

Akmal?"

Prince Kalib waves his hand dismissively. "Everyone knows that Akmal is a goat's anus. I don't have to purchase sixty yachts to prove that."

The situation is tense as everyone stares each other down.

Riley's words are still burning in my mind. *Manwhore. She really thinks that I'm still a manwhore?*

"Now let's put the business to rest and eat," Prince Kalib says. Just as he finishes the sentence, the servers come in with large trays that rattle with expensive china.

I should be happy. Riley is not getting her commission, which means that she's stuck with me.

But I'm not.

It breaks my heart that she's not going to become a pilot.

Her eyes are watery as she looks at me.

"I'm sorry," I mouth to her.

She just looks away.

I throw my napkin onto the table and stand up, ignoring all of the eyes on me.

Riley thinks I'm a manwhore; I'll show her what I'm truly capable of. I'll show her the real me.

I leave the room without looking back and take a left down the hall.

*Time to visit the harem.*

# CHAPTER TWENTY-TWO

## *RILEY*

My mouth is dry. I have heart palpitations and an empty feeling of dread in my stomach.

If Prince Kalib doesn't buy the yachts then I'll never be a pilot.

But worse.

I'll be stuck working with these sociopathic lunatics.

"Prince Kalib," I say, rubbing my sweaty palms on my skirt. "Imagine the worldwide press you'll get when reporters hear about this. You'll be known as the most charming and romantic man in the world. It will sound like a fairy tale."

He just shrugs.

Time to lay it on thick.

"It will go down in the history books as the greatest love story ever told. A handsome prince who was so in love with his harem of sixty women that he bought them each a yacht." That last part makes me throw up in my mouth a little bit.

"Forget the Taj Mahal," I continue. "Your story will take its place. You'll be the most coveted lover in history."

He tilts his head slightly as he thinks about it. "Nah," he says, crinkling his nose up. "I'd rather spend the money on myself."

Marv slams the contracts on the table, looking like he's going to tear the room up. Kara is still scowling at me. Dex is nowhere to be seen.

I don't know where he went, and I don't care. Actually, I'm insanely curious to know, but now is not the time. My six hundred thousand dollars and my future career as a pilot are on the line, and the line is extremely close to snapping.

"But it *will* be like spending money on yourself," I say. *Ugh.* I can hear the desperation in my voice. "Imagine how well your harem will treat you if you spoil them like this. Women find it so sexy when men lavishly spend money on them."

I have to stop myself from rolling my eyes at my own words. What I find sexy is a sideways look, a raised eyebrow, a flexed arm, a gentle touch, a private joke whispered into my ear, and a million other things that Dex has done over the past few days but had no idea he was doing.

I wish he was here. As much as I hate him right now, I still feel comforted when he's around. Even if he is a huge asshole.

The prince walks over and drops to a knee in front of me. "If you find money sexy, Mrs. Riley," he says, giving me the creeper vibe as he gazes up at me, "then I will shower you with gold coins and dry you off with one hundred-dollar bills."

He tries to take my hand, but I react fast, reaching for my wine glass instead. I down the rest of it.

"You misunderstood me," I say, leaning as far back in my chair as I can without falling over. "Grand gestures are romantic. Like purchasing sixty of the finest Gladstone yachts. And not only are they cost effective, they're sleek, elegant, versatile, and get great mileage." I don't even know what I'm saying anymore. Do yachts even have mileage?

"Kalib," Marv barks, standing up. "Last chance. Are you buying or what?"

The prince shakes his head. "Unfortunately, no."

I drop my head in defeat.

*Fuckfuckfuckfuckfuckfuckfuckfuckfuckfuckfuckfuckfuck.*

It's over.

I've lost everything.

My chance at being a pilot. My chance at a huge paycheck. My chance at working in the airline industry. My chance at love.

I'll let you guess which one hurts the most.

"Wonderful," Marv says. His tone suggests that it's anything but wonderful.

He tosses the contracts on the table and looks at his wife. "We're leaving. Now."

Voices ring down the hall as Kara gets up-lots of voices, like an approaching crowd.

All of our heads turn to the door as it gets louder. All of the voices are female. All of the voices sound extremely excited.

My heart stops when Dex walks back in. His eyes settle on mine first, and that determined look gives me goosebumps. He looks like he's determined to get me back. He's looking at me like I'm a challenge that he's never going to give up on.

And then I see what's behind him.

A crowd of beautiful half-naked women pouring in through the door.

And I'm back to wanting to throw up.

"Mr. Dex," Prince Kalib says, stepping back in shock. "This is highly inappropriate."

A stunning redhead squeals as she shuffles forward on stiletto heels. "Thank you so much!" She jumps on the prince and peppers his cheek with kisses. "My own yacht! I can't believe it!"

My mouth drops as the rest of the women scream, shout, cheer, squeal, and holler as they swarm into the room like a horny herd of lingerie models. They surround the prince, all talking at once, all thanking him for their new yachts.

The look on Prince Kalib's face is pure panic as he gets overrun by beautiful women. His heated eyes cut through the slathered-on makeup and over the top hairdos and lands on Dex.

Dex is standing there, staring back at him with a smug look on his face. "I told them the good news," he says coldly. "That they're each getting *a new yacht!*"

He shouts the last part like a game show host giving away the top prize, and all the girls scream in reaction.

I cover my ears as sixty women shriek around me, cringing as I expect the windows to shatter at any moment.

Prince Kalib starts biting his fingernails as the girls swoon around him. He tries to say something, but he stumbles over his own words.

Dex struts over to the table, giving me a wink

along the way, and grabs the contract. "And he's going to sign the contract now, in front of all of you!"

A new round of screeching rips through the room as Prince Kalib rubs the back of his neck, looking extremely uncomfortable.

Dex hands him the contracts. "Does anyone have a pen?"

Marv is at his side in the blink of an eye. "I have one right here," he says, holding up a golden pen.

The prince swallows hard as he reluctantly takes it. He's breathing heavily as all of the long-lashed eyes stare at him, brimming with excitement.

"I will sign it later," the prince says, his voice a little shaky. "After I read the contracts."

"Who wants to see the prince sign *right now?*" Dex shouts, getting the girls all amped up. They clap and cheer so loud that the prince gulps.

Prince Kalib glances at me quickly and then takes off the pen cap and signs the contracts. He looks a little stressed as he scribbles his name on the dotted lines.

My eyes land back on Dex (why do they always do that?) and I see him whispering something to Marv. The billionaire nods and then they shake hands. *What was that about?*

"There," Prince Kalib mutters, slamming the cap back on the pen as he grits his teeth.

"That's not all," Dex announces as he grabs Marv's phone off the table and waves it over his head. "The generous Prince Kalib would like to make it official right now! He's going to wire the money in front of all of you!"

The girls erupt like a sexy volcano, cheering as

they fight to get closer to the cringing prince. An Asian girl grabs him by the tie and pulls his tight lips onto hers.

Marv takes his phone back and sets up the three-way call between their banks. A minute later, Dex is holding the phone in the air, walking over to the prince.

"When the benevolent prince gives his approval," he shouts to the excited crowd, "you will each be the lucky owners of a brand-new luxury yacht. How does that sound?"

It sounds deafening. At least to me.

When the screaming dies down, Dex thrusts the phone into the prince's hands. Prince Kalib takes a deep breath as he holds the shaking phone to his ear.

"Hello." His voice is so shaky. I love it.

"Yes," he grunts, gulping after every word. "One hundred and twenty million." He turns increasingly pale with every second that passes. "I approve," he says, wiping his sweaty forehead with his hand.

There's complete silence in the room. Everyone is staring at him in stunned anticipation.

He nods, looking like he's going to throw up, and hands the phone back to Dex. "It's done."

The room explodes into cheers as the prince crumples to the floor, muttering something about how his father is going to murder him.

With all of the bodies jumping around in celebration, I somehow end up in Dex's arms.

Right where I belong.

He squeezes me as he lifts me off the ground like he's never going to let me go. "Congratulations," he whispers into my ear. "You're rich!"

I am rich. I have an utter fortune but it's not in my bank account. It's in my arms.

"You know that guy back there wasn't the real me, right?"

I squeeze him a little tighter to let him know that all is forgiven. It was an asshole move, but it's probably something I have to get used to with Dex. Being a bit of an asshole is part of his charm. And as long as he keeps his body nice and hard like this, I'm willing to let his occasional caveman actions slide.

Besides, he's got a really good heart under his hot, muscular exterior.

I know he loves me. I know he wouldn't do anything to hurt me anymore. I know he's the one for me.

So what's the point in fighting it?

Fate always gets her way.

She's a stubborn bitch.

Speaking of stubborn bitches, Kara is strutting over with a triumphant look on her face. "Great job, Dex," she says, grinning like a Bond villain. "You killed two birdies with one stone."

Dex pulls me protectively behind him as she approaches.

"You sold the yachts," she says, smiling wickedly. "But best of all. You got *her* fired!"

*Crappers.*

I forgot about that part.

# CHAPTER TWENTY-THREE

## *RILEY*

Remember that scene in *The Incredibles* where the father grabs the family under his arms in slow motion as he runs away from the explosion they caused? That's pretty much how we leave the island.

Marv has Kara over his shoulder, and he's practically dragging me and Dex behind him as he runs down the hallway in a panic.

"What the fuck, Marv?" Dex shouts, trying to remove his wrist from Marv's grasp.

Marv squeezes us even tighter as he runs. "We're getting out of here before he changes his mind!"

We don't stop running until we get to the plane. Marv yanks the stakes out of the ground with a savage grunt as Dex jumps inside.

"Get in," Dex says to me as he waves me over.

"What about the walk-arou—"

"Go!" Marv barks, giving me a look that has me sprinting to the passenger side of the plane.

"Why are we bringing *her?*" Kara asks as she glares at me. We're climbing into the airplane at the same time. "She doesn't even work for us anymore."

I just ignore her as Marv tosses the rope on the sand and opens the door.

"Wait!" Prince Kalib shouts as he runs down the path toward us.

Marv slams his door closed. "Go! Go! Go!"

Dex is a bit of a wild man, but he is a good pilot, and even he wouldn't leave without doing the necessary inside safety checks. He tries to do them quickly, but the prince catches up.

"Mr. Dex," he says, knocking on the window. "Please. A word."

"I can't hear you," Dex says, pointing to the headset covering his ear.

"I just spent over a hundred million dollars!" the prince shouts as he turns red. "You can give me thirty seconds of your time!"

Dex takes a deep breath and pulls out the key, placing it in my hand as he opens the door.

"Get the fuck back in here!" Marv shouts. "That's an order!"

He doesn't know who he's talking to. Dex doesn't take orders from anybody.

I try to ignore Marv's grumbling from the back as I lean toward the window, trying to hear what they're saying.

"That was a clever move," Prince Kalib admits. "I'm willing to tack on an extra million if you can make what we discussed a reality."

My stomach flutters. *What they discussed? What*

*did they discuss?*

I have a bad feeling that it somehow involves me.

"And what's that?" Dex asks, crossing his arms over his chest.

The prince looks uncomfortable. Anyone would look uncomfortable with a powerhouse like Dex staring them down like that.

"One night with your wife," he says with a gulp. "For one million dollars."

My mouth drops. *Am I worth that much?*

"No," Dex growls. "She's *mine* and only *mine*."

Dex turns back to the plane, but the prince doesn't know when to stop. He's used to getting everything he wants, so he probably doesn't recognize how close to getting punched he is right now.

"Five million."

Dex turns and cracks him in the face with a hard jab. His thunderous fist slams into the prince's royal nose and he falls on his ass, staring up at my man in shock.

"You want to make another offer?" Dex asks, stepping toward him with his hands squeezed into fists.

Prince Kalib shakes his head. Blood is trickling from his nose onto his chin.

"Good," Dex says, straightening back up. "You can't have everything in this world, Kalib. Riley is *mine*."

My heart is racing as Dex gets back into the plane. He puts the headset back on and starts the engine without saying a word.

I finally take a breath when we take-off and are flying away from the island.

*I guess I'm his.*

A smile breaks across my face as Dex levels the plane off.

I'm his, and he's not sharing me for anything.

He still hasn't said a word as he reaches out and takes my hand, giving it a little squeeze. My heart skips a beat.

I think I'm going to like being his.

Dex slows the engine when we're safely in the air, flying away from the island. I lean back in my seat and take a breath of relief as I watch him behind the controls, expertly maneuvering the plane.

He's wearing a tank top, and his large tattooed arms look simply beautiful as he moves them around, flicking switches and turning dials. I wish the back seats were empty so I could undo my seatbelt, lean over, and find out the true reason why this space is called a cockpit.

But unfortunately, we have company behind us.

The worst kind of company.

"Tell her," Kara says through the headset. She sounds like a snotty, spoiled brat. I look around for the red emergency lever that controls her seat, but unfortunately Cessnas don't come equipped with ejection seats.

"Tell her she's fired," Kara says, glaring beside her at Marv.

Marv is grinning widely as he stares out the window. His knee is bouncing up and down in excitement. Good for him. He can add another hundred and twenty million to the pile of money that he'll never get through.

"Marvin," Kara whines. "Tell her."

I hold my breath as Marv leans through the gap in the seats and pats my shoulder. "Great job back there, Riley. You too Dex."

"But…" I say, starting the sentence that I know he'll finish.

"But nothing," Marv says. "You'll get your commission, and you can keep your job."

"Really?" I ask, turning in shock. But it's not Marv that I look at, it's Dex. He's smiling contently as he flies.

"I see what you mean about her," Marv says, turning to Dex with a nod. "She is a clever one."

"And hot too," Dex says, shooting me a wink.

I swallow hard as I stare at his face, finally believing that he loves me. *Oh, my God.* That's so terrifying *and* exhilarating at the same time.

Dex loves me.

But of course he does. It's fate. I know that now.

No way can two polar opposites like us get together without a little nudge from lady fate. She may be a stubborn bitch, but if I ever meet her, I owe her a thank you.

"What?!?" Kara screams when she hears the news. "The yachts are sold. You're supposed to *fire* her!"

Marv just rolls his eyes, not looking back at his bitching wife.

"When you finish flight school," Marv continues, "you have a job as a pilot waiting for you with Gladstone Industries."

"Really?" I ask, whipping my head around. "A pilot?"

"Co-pilot," Dex corrects.

I grin at him and he gulps. "We'll see."

"Are you fucking kidding me?" Kara asks, clawing her husband's shoulder. "She's just a fuc—"

Dex smiles as he shuts off her mic.

"That's better," Marv says as we all take a breath of relief. Kara folds her arms across her chest and sits back down in her seat, sulking like a spoiled kid.

I can't stop grinning. I just got six hundred thousand dollars and a job as a pilot. Not to mention my sexy pilot boyfriend. Things are looking up for Riley!

"Are you sure you're okay with this?" I ask Dex. We'll be flying together everywhere. We're both control freaks, and I don't know how we're going to fly a plane with our two completely different styles, but I just know that it's going to work.

"You said it yourself," he answers with a grin. "The FAA requires that all jet air transport aircrafts have at least two pilots. I may be as smart and sexy as two people, but I'm still only one."

"Are you going to be able to share the controls?"

*This is going to be so much fun!*

He flicks off Marv's headset and I chuckle.

"Just remember," he says, turning to me with a heated stare. "In *my* cockpit, you follow *my* rules."

"*Our* cockpit," I correct, raising my chin in the

air. "*Our* rules."

"Better brace yourself."

"For what?"

He looks at me and smiles. "For some heavy turbulence."

# CHAPTER TWENTY-FOUR

## *RILEY*

"You can have these back," I say, slipping off the rings and placing them in Dex's palm. He looks surprisingly sad to see his fake marriage end in a fake divorce.

We're in a private hanger at the airport the next morning, about to go home. Marv's Bombardier Global 8000 jet is sitting behind me like a sleeping giant. As horrible as some of the moments were on this trip, I'm sad to see it end.

As low as the lows were, they were all worth it for the highs. Falling in love with Dex has raised me higher than that jet ever could.

"Okay," Dex says sadly. He slips the rings into his pocket and sighs. "These rings are cursed by the ice queen anyway. I'll give you real ones someday soon."

My chest flutters at his words. "Would you really marry me?"

His face is intensely serious. "In an instant."

I'm suddenly very aware of my own heartbeat. It's pounding.

"Would you say yes?"

"I don't know," I say, teasing him. "You'll have to ask me to find out."

"Maybe I will," he whispers as Marv and Kara enter the hangar.

Kara still looks pissed. I'm still here, which means that she didn't win, which means that she's throwing a temper tantrum, which means that I'm trying to hide my happy smile.

She storms past us without saying a word and marches up the stairs into the plane.

Marv walks over to us with a big smile on his face. He's still thrilled about the hundred and twenty million dollars he made. Not bad for a weekend's worth of work.

Dex warned me that by Wednesday he'll be back to his usual sour self.

"Check your online banking," he says to me with a grin.

My pulse is racing as I dig into my purse and pull out my phone. I thumb through my apps and sign into my bank while I hold my breath.

"Oh, my God," I whisper, staring at the screen with disbelieving eyes. It has to be some sort of trick. There are *way* too many zeroes on there.

"How much you got in there?" Dex asks, leaning over my shoulder.

"Six hundred thousand and thirty-six dollars," I say, still not blinking. The thirty-six dollars was all I had in there before. "Marv," I say, feeling dizzy as I look up at him. "I don't know how to thank you."

He shrugs his shoulders as he smiles at me. "Don't. You deserve it. I couldn't have made the sale without you two."

"Does that mean I have a surprise too?" Dex asks, pulling out his phone.

Marv bursts out laughing as Dex looks down at it with hopeful eyes. "Hell, no," Marv says, chuckling. "We made a deal, and I *never* go back on a deal."

Dex sighs as he shoves his phone back in his pocket. He steps beside me and wraps his arm around my shoulder. "I have all that I need here."

"Good," Marv says, turning toward the entrance of the plane. "Because you're not getting a cent from me! Now get this jet started. We have to get back home. I have a big deal in the works."

"Please tell me it's in Hawaii," Dex mutters.

"Close," Marv says, turning back with a grin. "Tajikistan."

"That's not close at all!" Dex complains. "Wait," he whispers to me. "Where's Tajikistan?"

I have no idea. But I'm about to find out.

"It's going to suck without you," Dex says with a sigh.

I smile as I watch Marv climb into the plane. "Maybe I'll tag along for one more trip before I leave for flight school."

"Really?" he asks, looking thrilled.

"Depends," I say, looking at him sideways. "Is there anything fun to do in Tajikistan, or are we going to be stuck in our room all week?"

"I think we'll be stuck in our hotel room all week."

"Perfect," I say with a wide grin. "Then I'll

*definitely* go."

We head to the plane and I stop Dex before he walks up the stairs. There's something I don't feel right about.

"I want to split the money with you."

"No way in hell."

"You earned it too," I argue. He did do half the work, and he was the one who finally got Prince Kalib to finalize the sale. "I want you to have half. You deserve a fortune too."

He looks me up and down with the most content look that I've ever seen on his face. "I have a fortune, Riley. A priceless fortune."

My cheeks heat up as my heart skips a beat. I feel the same way.

"I'll tell you what," he says, cupping my cheek as he steps in close. "Normally I would never agree to this, but you can buy dinner on our first official date."

I nod as he leans in and gives me a soft kiss on the lips.

"You got yourself a deal," I say, licking his delicious taste off my lips when he pulls away.

"Good," he says, taking my hand and walking me up the stairs into the plane. "Better bring it all because I'm going all out. I'm talking appetizers, steak, wine, dessert, and enough breadsticks to make you sick."

"As long as you don't get too full," I say with a raised eyebrow. "I want you nice and agile afterward."

He turns to me with a furrowed brow. "Putting out on the first date?" he asks with a smirk. "I didn't expect you to be the type."

"Is that going to be a problem for you?"

He laughs. "As you long as you still respect me in the morning."

"We'll see," I tease, laughing as we walk into the plane.

He gives me a kiss and grabs my ass before heading into the cockpit. I linger by the door and watch him as he sits down in the captain's chair and puts his hat on. He looks so damn hot in his pilot uniform as he takes command of the plane. I could watch him all day.

I reluctantly pry my eyes off of him and walk to the galley to prepare everything for take-off. About twenty minutes later, we're in the sky and flying back to LA.

I bring Marv his glass of scotch, purposely ignoring every nasty call that Kara throws my way, and then grab two champagne flutes that I fill with ginger ale.

Dex would rather have a beer, and although I've chilled out a lot on this trip, I'm still not about to give a pilot a beer while he's at work, especially if I'm in the plane.

"Thirsty?" I ask as I sneak into the cockpit. I place the two glasses on the middle console and slip into the co-pilot's chair.

"What do you think you're doing?" Dex asks, looking at me with a smirk. "That seat is reserved for a licensed, qualified pilot. FAA regulations."

"Yeah, well, someone has to keep an eye on you," I say, flicking off the switch for the seatbelt light that he missed.

"Hey," he says, jerking his head over. "I kept that on for a reason. I don't want Kara or Marv coming up here to bother me."

"Great idea," I say, flicking it back on. "What about me? Can I bother you?"

He chuckles as he looks out the windshield at the floating clouds. "You can always bother me."

"You might not say that when I retire this ridiculously tight stewardess uniform and become a pilot. You'll be the one getting the drinks for me soon."

"Don't count on it," he says with a playful grin.

"I'm counting."

"And that stewardess uniform is *way* too hot to be retired," he says, looking down at my legs. The short skirt is hiked up high on my thighs. This time I don't mind him looking. "You may not have to wear it to work, but we'll definitely make use of that in the bedroom."

"I can't wait," I say, getting wet just thinking about it.

"Then don't," he says, breathing heavily as he turns to me. "Come on over and help your sexy pilot out with his joystick."

I'm really tempted, but I'm not that wild and reckless. Yet.

Something tells me that Dex will get me there eventually.

"Remember," he growls. "*My* cockpit. *My* rules."

The clanking of approaching stiletto heels echoes from down the hall.

"Where the hell is my champagne?" Kara shouts. She's snarling in the entrance to the cockpit. Her eyes are pure evil as she glares at me.

She sees our two glasses of champagne and

snatches them off of the middle console. "The champagne is for us royals," she snaps. "You're the help. You drink water."

Dex grins at me. "Do you want to do the honors, or shall I?"

"Let's do it together," I say, grabbing hold of the yoke in front of me.

We both smile as we yank the yokes back, jerking the plane up toward outer space.

Kara screams as she flies back, doing a backward somersault as the two champagne flutes full of ginger ale spill all over her.

We're both laughing as we straighten the plane back up.

"Oops," I say, stifling my laugh as I look back at her. She's on her ass with her back against the wall, looking wide-eyed as sticky soda pours down her face. She's soaked.

"Didn't you see that the seatbelt sign is on?" I ask cheerily. She rushes forward, but I quickly grab the door handle and slam the door in her face.

She kicks, screams, scratches, and claws the locked door while I sit back and put my feet up on the window.

"I like this new Riley," Dex says, nodding in approval.

"What can I say?" I ask, grinning as I put my hands behind my head. "You taught me to embrace my inner bad girl."

He reaches his hand out to me and I hold it, smiling at him. I couldn't be happier than I am right now.

I'm in love with Dex.

I'm not fighting it anymore. I'm embracing it.

He has my heart, and instead of fighting for it back, I'm letting him keep it.

It's in his hands, right where it belongs.

"Is this what a happily ever after feels like?" Dex asks, smiling at me. He looks so happy and at peace. "Flying off into the horizon with the sun at our backs?"

"Straight out of a fairy tale," I say, squeezing his hand. "An X-rated fairy tale."

It was a joke, but it feels like the truth. I wouldn't trade places with any of the Disney princesses, and none of the princes have shit on Dex.

He smiles and then his face turns serious. "I'm really happy that I met you, Riley."

My cheeks flush as warmth radiates through my body.

"You've been my co-worker, my fake wife, my friend, my girlfriend, and I have loved you in each. You're the one for me, Riley. I know it through and through."

I still haven't said that I love him. Not because I don't feel it-I feel it radiating in every cell of my body-but because it wasn't the safe thing to do.

Fuck being safe. Fuck being cautious.

It's time for a little adventure.

"I love you too, Dex," I say, locking eyes on his baby blues.

"Yes," he says, squeezing his hand into a fist. "Does this mean I won?"

I laugh as I shake my head at him. "I think we both won."

He smiles and looks ahead. "I think you're right."

# EPILOGUE

## *DEX*

*A year and a half later...*

"You're in my seat."

"Correction," I say, grinning up at Dex as I stretch out in the Captain's chair. "It *was* your seat."

After an intense year of classes, non-stop practice, all-night study sessions, roughly sixteen hundred logged flight hours, and a whole lot of aced tests, I'm officially a licensed and certified Airline Transport Pilot.

And a damned good one.

"I like you better in your stewardess uniform," Dex says, still standing over me. "I miss that short skirt."

"I don't," I say with a laugh. "I hated showing the bottom of my ass cheeks every time I bent over. These pants are much more professional."

"Not if they're crumpled up on the floor," Dex says. *Uh-oh.* He's getting that look again; the one that he gets right before my clothes end up crumpled on the floor.

I swallow hard as I look out the windshield. We're in Marv's jet that's still in the hangar. It seems to be empty, but any airport personnel can walk in at any time.

"Don't get any ideas," I warn, feeling my heart speed up. "Marv will be here soon."

He looks at the watch that's strapped to his thick tattooed forearm and grins. "In an hour. We have time to settle this properly."

"Settle what?" I ask, feigning ignorance.

"Who gets the Captain's seat."

I make a show of looking down at the seat that I'm sitting on. "I think that's already settled, Mr. Co-Pilot."

He grumbles. This is killing him. I love it.

"Grab a seat," I say, pointing at the seat to my right. "*My* pussy pit. *My* rules."

He crosses his arms over his massive chest as he stares down at me. "I'm the more experienced pilot."

"Experienced at nearly crashing into the ocean," I say, looking out the windshield and trying to ignore his narrowed eyes on me. "I still remember that little incident."

"And I remember your naked ass being the cause of that little incident."

I shake my head. "I don't recall that part at all."

"How convenient."

"Agree to disagree."

"Agree to get out of my seat."

"Never."

We stare at each other for a full thirty seconds before either of say a word.

"Looks like the war is back on," I say with a grin.

"Was it ever off?"

I laugh. We've been dating for the past year and a half, and it's been ah-ma-zing. Although sometimes we are at each other's throats, we're always quick to make up in the best possible way: with hot make-up sex.

Three months after our trip to Prince Kalib's private island, we moved in together, and it's been a dream ever since. I bought a cute little house with the rest of the commission money, and we both love it.

Dex has been so supportive during my flight training, helping me out and pushing me to be better and better.

One night he took me flying, and we were practicing landings. I was so frustrated at how hard he was pushing me, and I blew up at him, saying he was being too hard on me.

"You're carrying the most precious thing in the world to me on any plane you fly," he snapped back at me. "Of course, I'm going to ride you as hard as I can."

I just smiled and tried again and again and again until I nailed the landing. Once I saw it through Dex's eyes, it made me work a little harder. He was helping me become the best pilot that I could be for selfish reasons. He wanted to keep me safe.

I completed my training two weeks ago, and Marv held up his word and gave me a job as a pilot.

This is our first flight together. I should have known we would be fighting before we even started the engines.

"We can settle this the hard way," Dex says, licking his lips. "Or the fun way."

"Ohh," I say, rubbing my chin while I look him up and down. "I want the fun and *hard* way." My eyes drop down to the front of his pants where he's hiding my favorite joystick.

He grins as he loosens his tie and starts unbuttoning his shirt. "That's why I love you," he says, biting his bottom lip as he stares down at me.

"What's going on here?" I ask, feeling my breath quicken as he takes off his shirt. "I wasn't trained for this during my flight courses."

"I hope not," he says, leaning over me. I hold my breath as he places his hands on my arm rests, flexing his tattooed arms as his lips hover over mine. "The pilot with the best control should be the Captain. The one who comes first moves to the co-pilot's seat."

"Mmmm," I moan, enjoying his hard body so close to mine. I'm already getting wet. I'm going to suck at this game.

But it's a competition I'm going to love to lose, so I agree.

His lips come down hard on mine, getting me all worked up. I love kissing Dex. His tongue is like a roller coaster-gliding, plunging, thrilling. And of course, it always gets my heart pumping.

We've had sex hundreds of times over the past year and a half, but each time keeps getting better and better. Dex has become a master at pleasing my body, knowing exactly where to touch at the right pressure and speed. That's why I'm probably going to be flying to Fiji in the co-pilot's seat.

Like I care.

Dex unbuckles his pants and lets them drop to his ankles. I gulp as I stare at the huge rod in his boxer briefs.

"So, I guess it's true that pilots get it up faster," I say, shifting in my seat.

He pulls his boxer briefs down and grips his hard dick, sliding his hand up and down his long shaft. "And we can keep it up for hours too."

"Prove it."

The two of us work together to get my clothes off as quickly as possible. He pushes me back down on the seat, and I spread my legs for him as he kneels in front of me and comes forward, gripping his massive cock.

"Watch this smooth precision approach," he says, grinning as he approaches.

I laugh until the head of his cock pushes against my opening, making me gasp. Then there are no more laughs. Just shivers of anticipation.

He fills me completely, burying his huge dick down my tunnel as he drives in deep. I'm not going to last long. I can already feel it.

The thrill of fucking in a cockpit with the added thrill of being in a hangar that anyone can walk into at any time is making the pressure build in my body quicker than usual.

Dex grabs my knees and separates them, staring down at his cock sliding in and out of my pussy. He reaches down and presses his thumb onto my aching clit, rubbing it in quick circles.

*Don't come. Don't come.*

I'm trying to last but the feeling is just too fucking amazing.

"No fair," I say, grabbing his wrist. I try to pull his hand away but it doesn't move. "Please assist yourself before assisting the people around you."

Dex grins, but he doesn't listen. He rubs my clit harder and it's enough to send me flying through the clouds. Who needs a pilot's license when Dex can bring me to these insane heights?

My muscles clench around him as the orgasm hits me. I'm crying out, cursing his name as the delicious waves of heat wash over me.

He grunts soon after, thrusting hard as he empties himself fully inside me. I open my arms and then wrap them around him as he falls into me, breathing hard and fast.

His cheek is pressed against my breast as he slips out of me. "You're in my seat."

"Are you sure you want it?" I ask, scratching his back. He loves it when I scratch his back after sex. "It's full of juices and cum. Maybe you should sit in the back with Marv."

He laughs. "And miss the spectacular view? No thanks."

"You can see the spectacular clouds from the passenger windows."

"That's not the spectacular view that I'm talking about."

The door of the hangar opens, and we explode out of each other's arms, getting dressed in record time. "What's going on in here?" Marv asks when he walks in the plane two minutes later.

"We just had sex," Dex says.

I slap his arm so hard, but I think I hurt my

hand more than I hurt him.

"That's not true," I say, my voice racing. "I was doing the necessary checks."

"That's right," Dex says with a smirk on his frustratingly handsome face. "She was checking out my cock."

Marv just rolls his eyes. "Save it for Fiji," he says. "You have two weeks on the beach with your own private villa."

"Really?" Dex asks, perking up. "No Motel Seven this time?"

Marv shakes his head as he heads into the fuselage. "Not this time. Only the best for my honeymoon."

Dex and I turn our heads slowly, smiling wide as we make eye contact.

"Beachfront," I whisper.

"Private villa," he whispers back.

We're about to high-five when the new bride walks into the plane. "Hi, guys," she says cheerily.

"Hi, Sandra," we both say back.

Thankfully, Kara is no longer in the picture. A month after we returned from Prince Kalib's private island, she got fired from Hidden Pleasures after she went on an angry rant on Twitter. She managed to insult overweight people and four different races in only a hundred and forty characters. There was a *huge* public backlash, and she hasn't been able to get a modeling job since. She and Marv divorced shortly after.

His new wife Sandra is awesome. I actually enjoy spending time with her, and she makes these trips even better.

"You two keep your eyes on the road and not

on each other, okay?" she says, smiling wide. "I don't want to crash on the way to my honeymoon."

"Don't worry," Dex says, smiling back at her. "I have big plans for this trip."

My cheeks heat up and I swallow hard as I think back to last week. I was searching for one of Dex's old t-shirts in his drawers when I found a purple box.

An engagement ring box.

I gasped, holding my breath and staring at it for a full five minutes. When I finally caught myself, I quickly closed the drawer and walked away. I didn't look inside, but I know what was in there. *I guess I'll find out for sure this week!*

I would love to marry Dex. He'd be an amazing husband and an excellent father. He's so excited to have kids, and although I've never really thought about it before we met, I haven't been able to stop thinking about it lately. I really want to have his children.

"Just get us there safely," Sandra says before walking back to join her new husband. "So we can have some fun on the beach!"

"All right," I say, reluctantly stepping out of the pilot's seat when we're alone again. "You have more control even if you did come only ten seconds after me. You can be the pilot."

"Sit that fine ass down," he says, grabbing the co-pilot's headset. "Do you really think I'm going to let you be the co-pilot on your first official flight? You're flying. You earned it!"

"Really?" I ask, feeling a dump of adrenaline rocket through me. "Are you sure?"

He grins as he puts his headset on and looks

ahead. "Awaiting your instructions, Captain."

I take a deep breath trying to calm my excited nerves. *So, this is what it's like to have all of your dreams come true.*

It's pretty fucking awesome.

I put my headset on, smiling wide as I turn the plane on. The engines rumble under my feet, and I have to bite my tongue to keep from squealing in joy.

The headsets click on, and I hear Dex's gravelly voice in my ear. "What can I do for you, Captain?"

I grin as I turn to him with raised eyebrows. "A coffee. Two milks."

His face drops. "Are you serious?"

"*My* cockpit. *My* rules."

He huffs out a frustrated breath as he gets up from his chair and heads into the galley. I slap his ass as he passes me. "The parachute's over there if you don't like it, sweetheart."

The look he gives me tells me I'm going to pay for that later.

I bit my lip and grin. I'm already looking forward to it.

# THE END

# WANT MORE RILEY AND DEX FOR FREE?

Join my newsletter for an exclusive extended epilogue by going to:
**www.authorkimberlyfox.com/newsletter.html**

Get the Exclusive Epilogue to see how Dex proposes. You won't believe how it goes all wrong and what he does to get Riley to say yes!

## Also by Kimberly Fox:

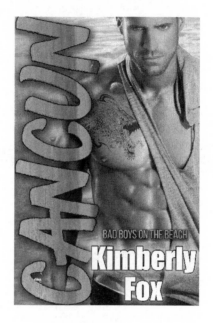

## Cancun

**"You need a rebound. They call me Mr. Trampoline."**

What happens in Cancun, unfortunately for my cheating boyfriend, doesn't stay in Cancun.

I caught him on the first night of our vacation balls deep in my worst enemy: the bitchy obnoxious girl who my best friend chose to be her maid of honor instead of me.

Now I'm stuck on this resort, in the same small room as my ex, until my friend gets married at the end of the week.

This place is a paradise but it feels like hell.

It's all going so wrong until I meet Ethan, the dirty talking bad boy with the body carved out of granite.

He's going to teach me what paradise is really about.

And it isn't sand and palm trees...

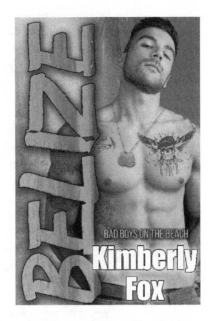

## Belize

**Cancun was hot. Belize is on fire!**

I hate him.

How many times do I have to say that until it sinks in?

How many times until I can get the image of his inked arms and ripped abs out of my head?

How many times?

Because I'm at a million and it's still not working.

And this filthy talking, muscular Navy SEAL who has his crosshairs set on me isn't backing down.

I won't be able to stand up to his hotness for long.

I'm ready to surrender and let him claim his spoils of war.

Me.

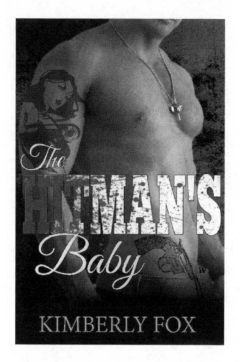

## The Hitman's Baby

**Nobody fucks harder than a girl that hates you. And this girl hates me. Hard. She's going to be fun.**

I hate guys like him.

So why am I always so attracted to his frustratingly arrogant and cocky type?

Well, his muscular, inked up arms aren't helping at all.

I should stay away from him.

I should leave.

He's more dangerous than just a killer smile.

But it's not like he'd ever untie me and let me walk out the door...

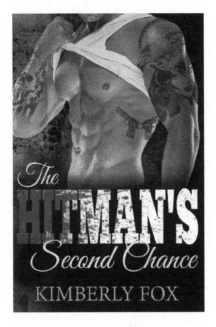

## The Hitman's Second Chance

**I lost her once and nothing is going to stop me from getting her back. Even her.**

Everyone deserves a second chance, but that doesn't mean I have to give Logan shit.

I should put a bullet in his heart for what he did to mine.

He didn't just break my heart. He ground it up into dog food and left it out for the vultures.

I was broken when he left.

It took a long time but I picked up the pieces and put my life back together.

But I'm in serious trouble and he's the only one who can help me.

And I'm afraid the pieces will all come crashing back down.